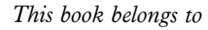

This book belongs to

....

CONTENTS

Edited by Thomas McBrien. *Designed by* Pritty Ramjee.
Cover illustrated by Stuart Trotter.
Endpapers illustrated by John Harrold.

THE
RUPERT.
ANNUAL

EXPRESS NEWSPAPERS

Farshore

First published in Great Britain 2021 by Farshore
An imprint of HarperCollins*Publishers*
1 London Bridge Street, London SE1 9GF
www.farshore.co.uk

HarperCollins*Publishers*
1st Floor, Watermarque Building, Ringsend Road
Dublin 4, Ireland

ISBN 978 0 7555 01069
Printed in Italy
001

RUPERT and

RUPERT SETS OUT TO PLAY

Says Mrs Bear, "It's cold today.
Keep moving, while you're out at play."

"Your Daddy's out of sorts," she sighs,
"Buy him a gift, some nice surprise."

"What's wrong with Daddy?" says Rupert to Mrs Bear. "I've just offered to tidy the garden shed, but he hardly answered. Is he ill?" "Not exactly ill," replies Mummy. "Just out of sorts. All he wants to do is sit quietly in his armchair." "Oh, then I'll help you with the washing-up instead," says Rupert promptly. When all the crockery has been washed and dried, he fetches his ball. "May I go out to play now?" he asks. "It's a good day for a game of football." "All right," says Mrs Bear, "and mind you keep warm." Just as Rupert is going Mummy calls him back and gives him a little money. "I think your Daddy needs cheering up," she smiles. "When you've had your game see if you can find anything in a shop that you think will please him, and buy it for a present." "Yes, I know the sort of shops to look at," says Rupert. "Goodbye, Mummy."

6

the HOUSEMOUSE

Shopping for presents can be fun, but Rupert and Rastus choose the wrong day for their jaunt to the Daisyham store. Luckily, they make a very useful friend, and from then on there is surprise after surprise for the two chums.

RUPERT CALLS BILL AND ALGY

Now Rupert, feeling cold and glum,
Is glad to see two playmates come.

He dashes forward, in fine form.
"Come on, you two, we must keep warm!"

Rupert carefully pockets the money that his Mummy has given him and trots away in search of some chums to make up a game of football. Finding the village green deserted, he wanders on until he reaches open ground beyond Nutwood. "My, it's colder than I thought," he murmurs, shivering in the raw air. "Perhaps they've all decided to stay indoors by their fire. I wonder if I'd better run straight away to find a shop and look for something to please Daddy. It will be better than standing about here." Just then he spies two of his best pals, Bill Badger and Algy Pug, and he quickly decides to have the game first. "Come on, you two!" he shouts. "We must get warm somehow. Where are the others?" "That's just what we were wondering," says Bill. "Good, you've brought a football, Rupert. Let's start our game and see if anyone joins us later on."

RUPERT BREAKS OFF THE GAME

"Look, here comes Rastus!" Algy beams.
"We can play football with two teams!"

The little mouse just walks straight by.
Bill calls, but there is no reply.

"He's deep in thought, I'll run along
And ask if there is something wrong."

"Sorry! I've something on my mind,
A gift for Granny I must find."

The three friends run about eagerly until they are all glowing with warmth. Then just as Rupert is trying to get the ball away from Bill, there is a shout from Algy Pug. "Look, here comes someone else. Now we can have a proper game, two-a-side." The newcomer is Rastus, the country mouse, and he is approaching slowly with his head bent in thought. "Hi, Rastus, we want you to join us and balance our game," Bill calls. To their surprise Rastus pays not the slightest attention and just walks steadily past them. "Well! What on earth's the matter with Rastus today?" Rupert exclaims. "Hi, Rastus! Won't you join our football?" At his approach Rastus jerks his head around. "Oh dear, did you call?" he says. "No, I'm no good at football; besides, I was thinking of something else. I've been sent out to choose a present for my Granny who has been ill and I've no idea what to buy her. What *do* Grannies like?" At his words Rupert starts and asks him to wait a minute.

RUPERT GOES WITH RASTUS

Says Rupert, "We must leave the fun,
We've both got shopping to be done."

Across the green the two pals race,
To Daisyham, a busy place.

"This shop sells bath salts, soap and such.
I don't think they'd cheer Daddy much."

Just then there comes an icy blast.
They shelter till the worst is past.

What Rastus has said reminds Rupert that it is high time he carried out his Mummy's errand and he turns back to Bill and Algy. "You two can go on playing with my ball, but don't lose it," he calls. "Look, here are two more pals coming to share the game. Rastus and I have both got orders to buy things at shops. We should not be away long." "Our own shops aren't very big. Let's go right across the common to Daisyham," says Rastus. So they set off and walk quickly in the cold air.

The two pals reach the village and wander through the streets. "I still don't know what sort of shop I want," says Rupert. "Here's one that sells scented soaps and bath salts. I don't think they would cheer my Daddy very much." "No, nor my Granny. She has already got plenty of those," says Rastus. They walk on feeling very cold, and at last they shelter beside a wall. "My, what a bitter wind!" mutters Rastus. "I was warm when we came but now I'm absolutely f-f-frozen."

RUPERT WONDERS WHAT TO BUY

They hurry on. "This shop seems best.
Look, it's far bigger than the rest."

Sighs Rupert, "Bedsocks, ties and shoes,
I simply can't think what to choose!"

"There's an assistant! Shall we ask
If she will help us with our task?"

"No, wait," says Rastus, "there's no need.
Books! *Everybody loves to read!"*

Rupert and Rastus are so cold that they dare not stand still any longer and they trot into the village square. "I say, here's a shop far bigger than the others," says Rupert. "It seems to sell everything. Let's go in." So they wander around the many full counters. "I'm lovely and warm in here," says Rastus happily, "but it's still hard to know what to buy. There's so much that I can't decide what to choose." "H'm, my trouble is that everything needs more money than I have," says Rupert. The problem is still worrying the two little pals as they explore the big store. "Let's ask that assistant when she has finished serving her customer," says Rupert. "She may know what would make a Daddy and a Granny happy." "Yes, and she may *not*," says Rastus gloomily. "She doesn't know *my* Granny!" All at once he has an idea. "Books!" he exclaims. "Everybody likes books. I wonder if there are any here." "Yes, I can see lots," says Rupert. And he leads the way to another counter.

RUPERT READS MANY BOOKS

*"I don't think we need her advice.
Let's peep in some; this one seems nice."*

*Says Rupert, "Here's a quiet nook
Where we can sit and have a look."*

*The pals collect a goodly pile,
Then sit and read for a quite a while.*

*When they get up to make their choice,
They cannot hear a single voice!*

The books on the counter all look so nice that Rupert and Rastus spend quite a long time trying to choose. "We can't buy any of them without knowing what's inside them," says Rastus. "Let's take one or two and see. My, they're rather heavy. Are there any chairs so that we can sit and read them?" They walk nervously around until Rupert spies a narrow way leading behind a counter. "Here's the spot," he murmurs. "We shall be quiet here and there are boxes to sit on." As Rupert had hoped, nobody interrupts the little pals in their hide-out. They peer into the books and become so interested that they creep out once or twice to bring more from the counter until there is quite a pile. "My, I have enjoyed this," says Rastus. "But I still don't know what Granny would like." "And I haven't even looked at the prices," says Rupert. "Come, we must put them all back." They carry them out. Then Rupert stops. "Can you hear anything?" he whispers.

RUPERT FINDS THE SHOP SHUT

Some counters now have covers on.
Frowns Rupert, "Everyone has gone!"

The frightened pals run to and fro.
"We're quite alone! Come on, let's go!"

But now a dreadful shock awaits!
The doors are locked, with iron gates!

Gasps Rupert, staring in dismay,
"It must be early closing day!"

Rastus stares at Rupert. "No, I can't hear anything," he says. "What should I hear? Can *you* hear anything?" "No, I can't," says Rupert. "That's what I don't like!" They hurry into the middle of the store. Some of the counters are covered with cloths, but there is no one to be seen. The two pals, now rather frightened, run this way and that. "Where on earth is everybody?" quavers Rastus. "We're alone!" Rupert pulls himself together. "I don't understand it at all," he says.

"The place was so full and now—nobody! If there are no assistants we can't buy anything for my Daddy and your Granny, so we'd better go too. Was this the way to the main entrance? Come on, let's hurry." Then a worse shock is in store for them, for the great doors are shut and padlocked, and between them and the street is drawn an iron grille. Rupert gazes in horror as he realises what has happened. The store is shut and they are alone. "It must be early closing day!" he gasps.

RUPERT SEARCHES EVERYWHERE

"We simply must get out somehow!"
Cries Rastus, in a panic now.

Scampering round, the pals are shocked
To find that every door is locked!

They pause, and Rastus Mouse despairs,
But Rupert says, "Let's try upstairs."

Soft scraping noises by their side
Make Rastus whisper, "Quick, let's hide!"

Rastus gazes in silence as he realises what has happened, and he looks as if he is going to cry. "Cheer up," Rupert sighs. "We are at least in a warm place instead of out in that freezing wind, but if it *is* early closing day, the shops won't open again until tomorrow morning. We *can't* stay away from home all that time." "Perhaps there's a back way out," Rastus suggests. And, leaving the main entrance, they scamper the other way, and try each door that they can find, but with no success. The two little pals hurry on feeling desperate. At length they pause for breath. "I suppose we should get into an awful row if we showed ourselves at one of the big windows and tried to call people outside," mutters Rastus. "We shouldn't be seen," says Rupert. "Didn't you notice the heavy blinds that they have let down? Let's go up to the next floor and see if we can get out there." They move off and are at the foot of the stairs when a scraping noise make them stop.

RUPERT MEETS A NEWCOMER

"Someone is coming! Hush, Let's peep!
Another mouse!" Then out they creep.

"Kenneth the housemouse is my name!
So you're shut in? I'm the same!"

"I'm jolly glad that you're about,"
Says Rupert. "How do we get out?"

"Get out?" The housemouse holds his sides.
"But I don't want to!" he confides.

In the silence of the empty shop the sudden scraping noise is so startling that the two little pals scuttle away and dodge behind a pillar. "A panel of the staircase was moving," whispers Rastus. "I don't like this a bit." Peeping out of their hiding-place they give a gasp. "Why, it's another *mouse*! Hello, have you been shut in too?" says Rupert, as he edges forward. "Shut in? Of course I'm shut in!" the newcomer grins. "I'm Kenneth, the housemouse. Have you got names too? Tell me."

"My, I'm glad we met you," says Rupert. "This is Rastus, the country mouse, and I'm Rupert Bear from Nutwood. We came to buy presents for his Granny and my Daddy, and the shop closed before we noticed. We're shut in! Isn't it awful! We can't get out. You don't look at all worried. You must know the way out. Where is it?" Kenneth sits down and laughs. "Get out?" he splutters. "You don't know your luck! Why on earth do you want to get out? I *don't*!"

RUPERT IS SHOWN A SECRET

"We live here in such happiness,
And hide ourselves where none can guess."

Then Rupert says, "But we can't stop!
Please show us how to leave the shop!"

"It's all locked up! But come with me,
My home's as comfy as can be!"

The sliding panel Kenneth shows.
"Just follow me!" Then in he goes.

Rupert is puzzled. "I don't understand," he says. "You're shut in just as we are. Why don't you want to get out?" "Why should I?" laughs Kenneth. "I live here! So do my brothers and sisters, but we never let ourselves be seen. On early closing days the whole shop is my home, and a lovely home it is!" "B-but we *must* go home," says Rupert anxiously. "My Mummy and Rastus's Granny will be worried." "Oh dear, I don't know the ways out," says Kenneth. "I have never troubled to look for them." Rastus and Rupert are as unhappy as ever, and wonder what else they can do to find their way home. "Oh, don't look so glum," says Kenneth. "You've no idea how comfy it is in here, plenty of room. Always warm, always plenty of left-over food that nobody wants." "But you can't live here. You'd be seen," exclaims Rupert. "Where did you appear from a few minutes ago?" For reply, Kenneth takes them back to where a panel has been pushed sideways.

RUPERT EXPLORES A PASSAGE

Says Rupert, "My, this place looks grim!"
But Rastus frowns, "Quick, follow him!"

"Keep up with us, at any cost,"
He call, "or you will soon get lost."

A kind of cupboard lies ahead.
"Why, it's a wardrobe! There's a bed!"

"That's right," says Rastus, with a grin,
"It's Kenneth's bedroom! Do come in!"

Kenneth the housemouse crawls into the dark space revealed by the panel and Rastus follows him. "I say, what is all this?" murmurs Rupert. "What a lot of room there is under these stairs. Is this where you live? There's not much light." "Come on in," says Rastus. "Kenneth says he has lots to show us. He's gone on ahead. We'd better follow quickly or he'll lose us." He hurries away and Rupert squeezes into the space and finds a way through to an uneven passage, very narrow and gloomy. Trying to follow the sound of the other's footsteps Rupert picks his way through the awkward, dusty passage. "Where on earth can this lead?" he thinks. "If this is Kenneth's home I don't think much of it!" Seeing a lighter patch ahead he makes better speed to another moving panel. "Hello, this leads into a big box," he mutters. "No, it's a wardrobe back in the shop!" He finds himself among lots of furniture. Rastus is before him, and Kenneth is perched on a new bed!

RUPERT DOESN'T WANT TO STAY

Laughs Kenneth, "The whole shop is ours,
On early closing days, for hours!"

He says, "Why don't you stay for good?
It's comfy here. I wish you would."

"Oh no, we can't forever roam
Around a shop! We must go home!"

Rupert will not agree, it's plain,
So Kenneth leads them on again.

Rupert crosses to where Kenneth is beginning to do gymnastics on a spring mattress. "Come on up here," says Kenneth, "it's lovely and bouncy." "I say, you can't do that!" cries Rupert. "Surely those are new beds. No one will buy them if you make them dirty." "Pooh, I always dust my shoes," says the housemouse, "I never dirty anything. And look at this armchair. Everything's comfy here. Now then, are you sure you won't give up that idea of going home?" Kenneth seems so happy about life inside the big shop, and Rastus is half inclined to take up his idea and join him, but Rupert won't hear of it. "Kenneth must be jolly clever to live here always without being found out," he says, "but we two *must* find a way out. Whatever would your Granny say if you never came home again!" "Oh well," sighs Kenneth. "You're funny people to want to go out of this warm shop into the cold air outside. I may be able to help you. Follow me again."

RUPERT LISTENS TO VOICES

The little bear drops to his knees,
"Voices!" he whispers. "Quiet, please!"

"My brothers and my sisters share
A lovely playroom under there."

"Now, don't you think it would be grand
To live with such a happy band?"

"No school, no lessons to attend,
No – hey, have I upset your friend?"

The housemouse sets off again on his curious journey through odd passages behind the shop walls, sometimes going up slopes and sometimes down, and the two little pals follow. All at once Rupert crouches near the floor to listen, and there Kenneth returns to find him. "What is it now?" says Kenneth. "Voices, several voices," says Rupert. "We aren't alone after all." "Of course we aren't," chuckles Kenneth. "There's a space under there that we use as our playroom. All my brothers and sisters are there!" Kenneth takes the two pals out of the narrow passage through another secret panel and into a parcels room. Then he tries again to persuade Rupert to live with him and all the other housemice. "You've heard how happy and jolly all my brothers and sisters are," he says. "You'd love it if you'd only stay here. And we'd love to have you too. There's plenty of room and plenty of food and . . . hello, what is your friend up to?" For Rastus is walking steadily away.

RUPERT KEEPS OUT OF SIGHT

"Someone is walking through the store,"
Says Rastus. "He'll unlock a door!"

"The watchman!" Kenneth grips his arm.
"Keep down! Don't dare give the alarm!"

"He simply must *not find us here.*
Keep quiet, till the coast is clear!"

Asks Rupert Bear, when all is still,
"If he won't let us out, who will?"

Rastus does not pause, and he is nearly out of the furniture department before the others catch him up. "Hi, where are you off to?" asks Kenneth. "I heard footsteps," says Rastus. "I'm sure there's somebody here. If there is, he can tell us how to get out of this shop." At that, Kenneth becomes furious, and grabbing Rastus's arm he drags him behind some chairs. "Be quiet," he hisses. "Don't make another sound. It's the watchman making his rounds. He *must* not find us here!" The sudden rough handling bewilders Rastus and he allows himself to be pushed into a shelter between some large chairs. All three little pals crouch silently, listening for the approach of the watchman. The footsteps come nearer, then the sounds pass by and fade away as the man moves to another department. "Whew, that was a near thing," murmurs Kenneth, as they tip-toe away. "That's all very well," says Rupert. "If he doesn't let us out, who will? We simply must get home."

RUPERT FOLLOWS KENNETH

"Why, me!" the housemouse says, with pride,
Then makes another panel slide.

They all creep through, to find themselves
Among strange meters, pipes and shelves.

"This trapdoor's open, so you can
Go through the roof! A clever plan!"

"The roof? But we are going down*!"*
Says Rupert, with a puzzled frown.

Kenneth quickly recovers his spirits. "So you're still determined to go away," he says. "I can't understand you. The store will be open again tomorrow. Meanwhile we can give you a lovely time, comfy beds, plenty to eat, and *why* go out into the cold air when it's so warm in here? Come on, I'll show you where all the warmth comes from." "What? Another sliding panel!" exclaims Rupert. Kenneth slips into it and the others follow. A minute later, when they look round, they find they are in a very different sort of corridor. Rupert and Rastus hear Kenneth give a satisfied little cry. "This trapdoor's open and ready for us," he says. "It would have been too heavy for us to lift. Now I can carry out an idea that I have had and let you both out through the roof." "Oh, do stop teasing us," says Rupert. "One doesn't go *downstairs* to reach the roof!" "That's what you think!" laughs Kenneth. He leads the way down to the boiler room.

RUPERT HAS A LONG CLIMB

"That man-hole leads into our yard,
But lifting it would prove too hard."

"We'll go up to the roof instead,"
And Kenneth scrambles on ahead.

Gasps Rupert, "My, those pipes were hot!"
He's puffed, but Rastus Mouse is not!

Then struggling through that space somehow,
He pants, "A great long staircase now!"

A little further on Rupert and Rastus find Kenneth standing by a huge heap of coal and gazing upwards. "You might have got out that way into our courtyard but we couldn't lift that heavy man-hole," he says. "So that is the roof we were to go through, is it?" says Rupert. "No, it wasn't, that was only a sudden idea," chuckles Kenneth. "Now we'll really go to the roof." He turns the corner and, while Rupert and Rastus watch, he begins scrambling lightly up the wall by the pipes. Then follows one of the strangest climbs Rupert has ever done. "My, this is dangerous!" he puffs as he reaches a space high up in the wall and sees Rastus waiting for him. "I always heard that you mice could make your way all over a house without anybody knowing how, but this is the limit. Some of those pipes were hot. Thank goodness I have gloves on." Struggling into the space he squeezes through just in time to see Kenneth running up narrow stairs between two walls.

RUPERT MAKES A PROMISE

At last, although the way is rough,
They reach the attic, sure enough.

Says Kenneth, "Promise faithfully
That you will never tell on me!"

"Some bricks have gone; right through this wall
Into the next shop you can crawl!"

First Rupert scrambles through that space,
Into a kind of storage place.

Rupert arrives at the top of the narrow flight. "And where are we now?" he says breathlessly. "Why, this surely is the attic at last. Look at those beams and rafters. We must be just under the slates. Where's Kenneth? What does he want us to do? Is he going to take a slate off and let us out on to the roof?" "Here I am," Kenneth calls from the other end of the roof space. "If I show you the way will you promise never to tell anybody about my sliding panels and things?" Rupert and Rastus are so keen to get home that they give Kenneth their promise at once. "Even if I tell my Mummy about you," says Rupert, "I'll never say how you make your secret way around the store." "Right, then I'll show you your way," says Kenneth. "Just round here is the wall between us and the next shop. Some of the bricks have fallen away leaving a space. Go through and you will be next door." Rupert does not waste a moment, and quickly goes to explore.

RUPERT LOWERS THE LADDER

"We're in the next-door attic room,"
Says Rupert, peering through the gloom.

A double ladder, lying flat,
Makes Rupert murmur, "Fancy that!"

"Let's see if I can lift this thing.
Oh, my! Just look what's happening!"

Downwards a kind of trapdoor tips,
And into place the ladder slips.

Kenneth will not leave his own store and, saying goodbye, he returns the way he came while Rastus joins Rupert. "I wonder what sort of shop we're in now?" says Rastus. "It smells different from the store." "Yes, and I wonder if we're any better off," says Rupert. "It's still early closing and I expect this shop is shut too. Hello, here's a ladder. It's a double one. What can it be used for so close under the roof?" There seems to be no staircase or any way out of the next-door attic in which the two friends find themselves, and Rastus gazes inquisitively at the double ladder. "It looks new. I wonder if it's heavy," he murmurs. "Let's try it and see," says Rupert. He lifts one end and to their amazement a section of the floor tilts gently downwards. The top half of the ladder slides silently down into position. Rupert and Rastus look through the hole, and find themselves gazing at the upper floor of the shop below them. "So that's how it works," says Rastus.

RUPERT CREEPS DOWNSTAIRS

The chums climb down, then gladly spy
A proper flight of stairs nearby.

"Someone is calling," Rastus fears.
Down through the banisters he peers.

They find a garden store downstairs.
"It's open!" Rupert Bear declares.

Next moment, Rastus tugs his sleeve.
"That's just an office! Quick, let's leave!"

The ladder leading from the roof is so well oiled that it doesn't make a sound as it slides into position and the two pals descend quietly and look around. "There's no sign of anyone else on this floor," whispers Rupert. "I wonder if this shop is shut too, just as the big store was. We'd better go down further and find out." They reach a staircase and peer down to the ground floor before moving further. "I thought I heard a noise," breathes Rastus. "Listen to see if it comes again." The two pals creep very carefully down the stairs, and pulling aside a curtain Rupert finds himself behind a counter. "This is the shop," he murmurs. "It's all full of seeds and bulbs and flowerpots and garden things." Rastus joins him. "We're in luck," he says, forgetting to talk quietly. "Look, look, I do believe the front door is open. We're free! We can go home!" He grabs Rupert's arm, but the little bear turns to an inner door and pauses. "Come *on!* Why stay?" cries Rastus.

RUPERT SEES A SHOPMAN

"Someone is calling!" Rupert taps,
"We should see who it is, perhaps."

A weak voice answers Rupert's knock,
He enters, and receives a shock.

"I've fallen, and can't use my legs,
Please run for help!" the shopman begs.

An ambulance is what they need!
And Rupert dashes out, at speed.

Rupert bends toward the door leading inward from the shop. "Before we came down here you thought you heard a sound," he whispers. "Well, I can hear something now. It's in this room. Somebody's calling. He sounds unhappy. D'you think we'd better see who it is?" He knocks, and a weak voice tells him to come in. Opening the door he looks in and finds a nice office. Very quietly and carefully he looks further round the door and then he gives a start, for someone is half sitting and half lying on the floor. The figure is an oldish gentleman who shows his great excitement at the appearance of the two pals. "Oh, I am so glad to see you!" he exclaims. "I kept hoping some customers would come in and hear me calling and here you are! I was putting papers away before closing my shop – it's early closing, you know – and I twisted my leg badly. I need a doctor or an ambulance." "I'll see what I can do," says Rupert, as he dashes into the street.

RUPERT STOPS A POLICEMAN

He races down the busy street,
And tells a policeman on his beat.

Says Rupert Bear, "That policeman's kind,
He'll see to everything, you'll find."

"An ambulance is on its way,
Now, why did you come here today?"

"By helping me you've been delayed
In buying presents, I'm afraid."

Rupert runs along the pavement. "Daddy always says that if we are in trouble we must find a policeman," he thinks. "There's one over there. I'll tell him what happened." The officer listens solemnly and then wastes no time in going to the shop. As he enters the office Rastus comes out. "Did you tell the shopkeeper how we got into his shop?" asks Rupert. "No, I'd no chance," says Rastus. "He's so pleased to see us that he wouldn't stop talking. I just couldn't get a word in!" After some minutes the policeman comes striding out to fetch an ambulance, and entering the office again the two pals see that the old man is comfortable on the couch. "Now then, tell me," he smiles, "what did you two come here for?" "Well we started out to find a present for my Daddy and Rastus's Granny," says Rupert, "but we . . ." The shopkeeper interrupts him. "There's a pencil and paper on that table," he says. "I want your name and address, so please write them down."

RUPERT'S JOURNEY IS SLOW

Quite soon, an ambulance arrives,
Watched by the pals, away it drives.

Cries Rupert, "My, it's getting late!"
They make for home at such a rate.

The sun is setting in the west,
When Rastus gasps, "I'll have to rest!"

They stumble on, as darkness falls,
"Look, there's the village!" Rupert calls.

The old shopman folds the paper and puts it in his pocket and before the ambulance arrives he talks happily and endlessly, giving Rupert no chance to tell of the strange way by which he and Rastus entered the shop by its roof space. At length the policeman and the two pals watch the ambulance driving away and Rupert pulls himself together. "We've been out for *hours*," he cries. "We've found no presents, but we must hurry home." And they set off up the long slope onto the Common. "I'm not sure I know the way," says Rupert. "So we'd better not pause. Daylight won't last much longer." "I can't keep this up," gasps Rastus and, in spite of Rupert's anxiety, he insists on having a rest, so that the light has faded before they cross the top. Now in the gloom the long grass makes the little mouse stumble about and they are forced to go more slowly. When at last they can just spy the distant village, darkness has fallen.

RUPERT READS THE LETTER

"At last, you're back! How glad I am!
Where have you been? To Daisyham!"

"This note and parcel came from there,
By motor-bike!" says Mrs Bear.

"It's from that shopman, just to tell
His injured leg will soon be well!"

"He's sent round presents, by his son,
To thank us both for all we've done!"

Mrs Bear is waiting anxiously. "Where *have* you been?" she demands. "Algy brought your ball back ages ago." "Oh, Mummy, we're dreadfully tired," exclaims Rupert. "We went to Daisyham and we've been simply hours coming back, stumbling through hedges and . . ." "Did you say Daisyham?" says Mrs Bear. "A boy on a motor-bike came from there barely ten minutes ago. He brought something for you. Look!" On the table Rupert sees a parcel with an envelope under the string.

Completely mystified by the parcel Rupert takes off his gloves and opens the letter. "Look here, Rastus," he cries as he reads it. "This is from the old shopman who went away to hospital. He says they put his leg right quickly and he is so pleased that he has sent his son round at once with presents." "Whatever are you talking about? What shopman?" asks Mrs Bear. "Here, Mummy, you read it," exclaims Rupert. "We'll tell you, but please let us open the parcel first."

RUPERT SHOWS A LOVELY GIFT

With lily bulbs those trays are filled,
No wonder both the chums are thrilled!

Cries Rupert, "Daddy's gift has come!"
"So has my Granny's," laughs his chum.

So Rupert shows the lovely gift,
And hopes that Daddy's gloom will lift.

"Late lily bulbs! It can't be true!"
He murmurs. "A whole box full, too."

Rupert can hardly wait to pull the paper and the string off the parcel and soon the little pals are gazing at two flat boxes containing some round brown things and a lot of straw. "What are they?" says Rupert. "They look like onions." "They don't smell like onions," says Rastus. "Just a moment, here's another letter in the same handwriting," says Rupert. "Whew, just listen to this! They're late lily bulbs, very rare. Presents for my Daddy and your Granny. Do look, Mummy. D'you think these will cheer Daddy up and make him feel better?" Mrs Bear tells Rupert to go straight in to his Daddy. "He's no better," she whispers. "He's grumpier than ever because you were so late in coming come." So Rupert goes in quietly. "Look Daddy," he says. "Would you like these? They're late lily bulbs, very rare." Mr Bear seems prepared to scold him. Then he picks up one of the bulbs. "I've heard of these," he smiles, "but I've never seen any, and now here's a box full!"

RUPERT'S CHUM GOES HOME

Now Daddy, feeling fine once more,
Makes gaily for the cottage door.

"I'll carry home this sleepyhead,"
He smiles. "It's time he was in bed."

"That was the perfect gift, it seems,
And here's your money!" Rupert beams.

When Mr Bear returns that night,
The tale is told with great delight.

Mr Bear loves his garden, and the sight of the rare bulbs has quite driven away his grumpiness, so that he moves about more actively. "That box is for you, and Rastus is taking another one to his Granny," says Rupert. "Eh, what? Is Rastus *here*?" exclaims Daddy. "It's time he *was* in bed." Mr Bear, now full of smiles, packs the second box of bulbs and prepares to carry tired Rastus home. Mrs Bear is delighted. "You *were* clever to choose just the right present!" she smiles. "I didn't choose it, and it didn't cost anything," laughs Rupert. "See, here's the money you gave me!" He is hardly in bed before his Daddy comes in. "That young Rastus has been telling me a most amazing story," says Mr Bear. "All about being shut in a big store with a housemouse, and a journey through the roof, and an old shopman and . . ." "Yes, it *was* amazing and it's all true," cries Rupert. And he refuses to go to sleep until he has told his story all over again.

RUPERT'S FLOWER PUZZLE

In the story of Rupert and the Housemouse the little bear's Daddy receives an unexpected present of rare bulbs. Some bulbs are not rare at all and are in most people's gardens. Here are fifteen different flowers that Rupert has seen, either in gardens or growing wild on Nutwood Common. Can you tell what they are all called? And then can you pick out those that belong to the bulb family?

When you have made your list, compare it with the answers given below. Score one point for each flower you name correctly and two more points every time you pick out one of the bulbs.

ANSWERS: The flowers are: Foxglove, Bluebell, Tulip, Fuchsia, Poppy, Cyclamen, Sunflower, Rose, Iris, Snowdrop, Daffodil, Lily of the Valley, Cornflower, Crocus, Thistle. Among them are seven flowers of the bulb family: Bluebell, Tulip, Snowdrop, Daffodil, Cyclamen, Crocus and Iris.

RUPERT

"Who is that new boy over there
All by himself?" asks Rupert Bear.

Rupert is nearly late for school. Dr. Chimp is calling everyone in as he hurries into the playground. By the wall he sees a strange boy. "Who's he?" he asks Bill Badger as they file into class. "Don't know," Bill says. "He just stood by himself." Then Dr. Chimp comes in with the boy, a not very friendly looking lad in a kilt. "This is the Squire's grandson Hamish who comes from Scotland," Dr. Chimp says.

and HAMISH

"Hamish is Scots. He's here to stay
With Squire – a sort of holiday."

"To make friends, Bill I thought I'd try.
But he ran off. Perhaps he's shy."

Hamish, it seems, is visiting his grandfather and is to attend the school while he is here. He doesn't look pleased about it, neither smiling nor talking. "Probably shy," Rupert tells Bill. "Let's make friends after school." But after school Hamish hurries away. The pals go after him and catch up by the river. "Would you like to play," Rupert begins. "No," the boy says in a cold voice and turns away.

"Hey, Hamish, would you like to play?"
"No!" snaps the boy and turns away.

John Harrold.

RUPERT TRIES TO MAKE FRIENDS

*"He can't have meant to sound so rude.
I'm sure he's just misunderstood."*

*"Let's look for him tomorrow then,
And try to make friends once again."*

*They look all over, then he's spied
Loitering by the riverside.*

*"We need one more to play and thought
Of you." He says he'd rather not.*

Bill is having tea with Rupert and as they eat, they tell Mrs Bear about Hamish. "He really is awfully rude," Bill says. "He didn't talk to anyone at school and when Rupert and I tried to make friends he walked away." "Oh, dear," Mrs Bear says, "you must have misunderstood each other. Do try again. Make him feel you need him." The pals agree and as Bill leaves, Rupert calls, "Let's invite him to join a game of football with us all tomorrow."

Next day Rupert and Bill tell their pals about their plan. "I'm sure he'll join in if we say we really need him to make up sides," Rupert explains. Edward Trunk, Algy and Bingo aren't so sure, but agree when Rupert says that Hamish is probably just shy. So off they go in search of him and once more find him by the river, loitering. "We need someone to make up sides for football," Rupert greets him. "No thanks," Hamish grunts and turns away.

RUPERT THINKS OF A PLAN

"I'm sure he's lonely. Do try, dear,
To make him feel he's needed here."

Then later as he lies in bed,
A plan comes into Rupert's head.

For Rupert's plan they need a raft,
And this old door will be their craft.

He haunts the river so, this boy.
They plan to use it for their ploy.

"Well, did you try to make Hamish feel he's needed?" Mrs Bear asks Rupert at bedtime. He sighs: "We did try." And he goes on to tell how they found him and told him he was needed to make up sides for football. "But he refused – and rudely," Rupert winds up. "He seems to want only to loaf about by the river." "Be a dear and try once more," pleads Mrs Bear. "I'm sure he's lonely." Of course, Rupert agrees, and later in bed he thinks of a plan.

"Your idea better work after all this," Bill pants as Rupert and he carry an old door from his garden shed next day. "Sure to," Rupert says. "Since Hamish seems so fond of the river, we'll use it. If he thinks we're in danger, drifting away on a raft, he'll rescue us and we'll have shown him he's needed. This door's our raft." So a little later the pals are hiding by the river waiting for Hamish. "Here he comes," whispers Rupert. "Get ready to launch!"

RUPERT'S PLAN GOES WRONG

*"We'll make him think that we're afraid,
Adrift, and badly need his aid."*

*Their cries make Hamish start and stare
As if dismayed to see them there.*

*But what's this? They're gathering speed!
Now someone's help they really need!*

*Then down the towpath Hamish flies.
"I'll get you at the bridge!" he cries.*

When Rupert thinks Hamish is near enough he whispers, "Into the water with it, Bill!" They push the door-raft clear of the bank and jump on board. The raft drifts to the middle of the river. Hamish is now quite close but he seems sunk in thought. Bill nods to Rupert. "Help!" they yell. "We're adrift! Save us!" Startled, Hamish looks up. But he doesn't rush to the rescue as Rupert expected. Instead, he stares as if dismayed to see anyone there!

The pals try again. Sounding really quite frightened, they cry, "Please help us, please!" Then something happens that really does scare them. The raft begins to gather speed, cutting faster and faster through the water like a motorboat. But now Hamish springs into action. "Hang on!" he yells and races along the bank after them. "I'm going to try to stop you at the bridge." But hard as he runs, the raft seems to be drawing away from him.

RUPERT IS BAFFLED

But Hamish gets there just too late.
The raft has moved at such a rate.

"Shooglie!" the pals hear Hamish call.
They stop so hard they nearly fall.

More strange words are by Hamish cried.
The raft moves gently to the side.

"I can't explain this now, I fear.
But after supper meet me here."

"Oh, what's happening?" Bill wails as Rupert and he try hard not to fall off the speeding raft. They can see Hamish racing along the bank, but the bridge is looming over them and Hamish has hardly reached it. The raft sweeps under the bridge and is quite a way downstream when Hamish appears on the bridge. He shouts something. It sounds like "Shooglie!" And to the utter amazement of the pals the raft stops at once almost throwing them off.

Then from the bridge Hamish shouts again. But the pals can't understand the words. To their astonishment the raft moves gently to the bank where Hamish runs to help them off. "How did you do that?" Rupert gasps. Hamish shakes his head. But the pals keep on at him until he says, "Look, I can't tell you now. But, if you can keep a secret, meet me here after supper tonight and I shall explain then, right?" The very puzzled pals agree.

RUPERT MEETS SHOOGLIE

Hamish has brought a bucket when
He meets up with the pals again.

He calls out and before their eyes
The strangest creature starts to rise.

"We're such good friends at home that he
Has followed me down here by sea."

"His name is Shooglie and he dotes
On plain old-fashioned porridge oats."

After supper Rupert and Bill make their way to the riverside as arranged. Hamish arrives just after them carrying a big wooden bucket. "What's that for?" Bill asks. "You'll see in a moment," Hamish says mysteriously. "But first you must promise to keep secret anything I tell you and anything you see." The pals promise. Hamish turns to the river. "Shooglie!" he calls. For a moment nothing stirs in the dark water then Rupert and Bill cry out at what they see.

No wonder! For from the river rises a huge creature. Balanced on its back is the door-raft. "This is my good friend Shooglie, the Loch Shoogle monster," Hamish announces. Shooglie smiles. Hamish goes on: "When your raft took off today I guessed it had got stuck on Shooglie's spikes. So I stopped him and told him in our old Scots language not to show himself." Now Hamish holds up the big wooden bucket. "Here's your supper, Shooglie," he smiles. "Oats!"

RUPERT IS TAKEN BY SURPRISE

*"I tried to hide him. 'Twas hard luck
That on his spikes your raft got stuck."*

*Hamish is saying, "Now you see . . ."
A beam of light falls on the three.*

*It's P.C. Growler and it's clear
He doesn't know that Shooglie's here.*

*Then he looks up! "What's that?" he cries.
"Hamish's friend," Rupert replies.*

While Shooglie tucks into his supper and the pals lift the raft from his back, Hamish explains: "Shooglie was a baby when I found him near Loch Shoogle where I live. He was lost. So I took care of him in secret and we became great chums. When I came to visit Grandpa here Shooglie decided to follow by sea and river. I didn't think people would understand about him . . ."

"And that's why you kept near the river!" Rupert cries. Just then a bright light falls on the three and a voice says, "What are you lot up to so late?" It's P.C. Growler! What's more, it's plain he has not noticed the creature in the river behind them. All three start to talk at once. "One at a time," Growler is saying when he looks up. "W-what's that?" he gasps in horror. "It's a friend of ours – or rather, of Hamish," Rupert says. "His name's Shooglie and he comes from Scotland." Shooglie lowers his great head and smiles into Growler's horrified face.

RUPERT SAVES THE POLICEMAN

"Your grandfather the Squire shall hear
About this business, have no fear."

Next moment Growler's hanging by
His belt from Shooglie's jaws up high.

"Oh, do make Shooglie let him go!
It only makes things worse, you know."

"That monster creature and you three
Had better come along with me."

As soon as the policeman has got over his shock he addresses Hamish: "Did you bring this here?" "In a way I suppose I did," Hamish says. "And does your grandfather know about this?" Growler goes on sternly. "Well, not really," Hamish admits. "Thought so!" Growler says. "I think you'll all come with me." He puts a hand on Hamish's shoulder and – whoops! – next moment he is hanging by his belt from Shooglie's jaws. And Shooglie isn't smiling now.

"Make it put me down!" Growler cries. But Hamish folds his arms and declares, "Shooglie does not like to see people lay hands on me." "I didn't lay hands on you!" protests Growler. "I only touched you on the shoulder." "Please tell Shooglie to put him down," Rupert pleads. "It will only make things worse if you don't." Grudgingly Hamish agrees and next minute the three youngsters and Shooglie are being led off to Nutwood's police station.

RUPERT GOES WITH GROWLER

He's much too big to go inside
So to a clothes pole Shooglie's tied.

"The Squire is still not home you say?
Well, we can have the lad to stay."

"Too far to take you home tonight.
So you stay here. You'll be all right."

As off they go, they don't see that
A hot coal's landed on the mat.

At the police station, which is also Growler's home, Shooglie is left outside. Rupert and the others are led indoors. The policeman tells Bill and Rupert, "I'll take you two home after I've phoned the Squire and asked him to collect his grandson." But when he telephones, he learns that the Squire has had to go to the city and won't be back until late. He has taken the car so his housekeeper can't fetch Hamish. Mrs Growler who has come to see what's up, speaks: "Hamish can share our children's room tonight."

So that takes care of Hamish for the night. As kind Mrs Growler ushers him upstairs her husband tells him, "Your grandfather will come for you in the morning and we'll see then what he thinks of you bringing nasty monsters to our nice quiet village." Then he turns to Rupert and Bill. "Now I'll take you home." He leads them out but as they go something happens that no one sees. A hot coal jumps from the living room fire onto the hearth rug.

RUPERT SPOTS A BLAZE

"Oh, P.C. Growler, see that glare!
A house must be on fire back there!"

"It's my house!" Growler gives a shout.
"Let's pray they've all got safely out."

The whole downstairs is blazing when
They reach the Growler home again.

Then round the back they dash – and stare!
The "monster fire escape" is there!

As P.C. Growler takes Bill and Rupert to their homes he grumbles about "youngsters who ought to be safe in bed, not larking about with nasty great monsters". Then something makes Rupert turn round. "Look!" he cries. "Something's on fire!" The others swing round to see a glow in the sky. "It must be a house," Bill says. "It's mine!" cries Growler. "Quick! Back to the police station. My family are there and so's your friend." The three start to run.

When they reach the police station, they are stopped in their tracks by what they see. The ground floor is blazing fiercely. "My family and the lad!" Growler cries. "Trapped upstairs!" The three dash to the back of the building to see if there's any way in there. What a scene greets them! Shooglie has stretched his neck up to the window like a fire escape and Mrs Growler is sliding to safety down it. The others are safe on the ground.

RUPERT SEES SHOOGLIE RETURN

Then off darts Shooglie through the gate.
"No, no!" cries Growler. "Do please wait!"

"The Fire Brigade's too far from here.
The whole place will burn down, I fear!"

"It's Shooglie coming back! I say,
He's coming from the river way."

He puckers up his lips and blows
As well as any fireman's hose!

"Clever creature!" Growler exclaims. "Not a nasty great monster, after all!" laughs Rupert. Then without warning Shooglie races off through the police station gate. "Come back!" Growler yells. "You're not going to get into trouble!" But Shooglie has vanished into the darkness towards the river and Growler is too concerned about the fire to follow him. "We'll never get this out on our own," he groans. "And the Fire Brigade couldn't get from Nutchester in time."

Rupert, who can't believe that Shooglie who has been so brave and clever would run away, wanders out into the road and looks towards the river. Suddenly he hears something heavy moving fast and out of the darkness bounds Shooglie. The monster dashes up to the building, points his head at the flames, puckers his lips and blows a jet of river water into the heart of the fire, putting it out at once. Growler shakes his head in amazement - and admiration.

RUPERT MAKES A JOKE

Says Growler, "I'm ashamed to say
I thought that you had run away."

"The Growlers must stay with me then
Until their house is fit again."

Soon Hamish must be leaving so
Shooglie decides that he will go.

"If only Shooglie could have stayed
He might have been our Fire Brigade!"

Shooglie is a hero. P.C. Growler pats his head and says, "To think I imagined you'd run away when all the time you'd gone to get water. I am truly sorry." Just then there turns up the Old Professor who has seen the fire from his tower and come to see if he can be of help. When he hears all that has happened, he says, "The Growlers must stay with me until their home is repaired. And Shooglie shall have the use of my private lake until he goes home."

At last it gets near the day for Hamish to go home. Shooglie decides to leave first to be there to greet him. His new friends, including the Squire, come to say goodbye. "On behalf of everyone in Nutwood I thank you, Shooglie," the Squire declares. Shooglie smiles at everyone then starts down the river towards the sea. As he watches him go Rupert chuckles: "It's a pity he can't stay. Think what a splendid village fire engine he'd make." The End.

MAKE A CHRISTMAS TREE
JUST LIKE RUPERT'S

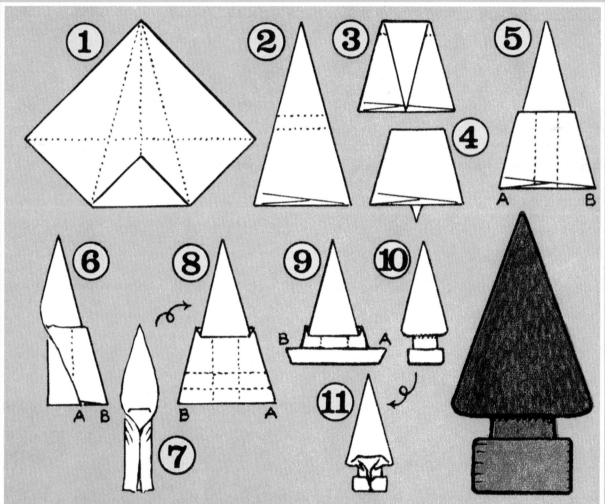

You will need a square of thin paper. Fold opposite corners together each way to find the middle and fold one corner part way to the centre (Fig. 1). Fold both sides in along the sloping dotted lines (Fig. 2), note the new dotted lines and bring the top point to the middle of the bottom edge to give the upper crease (Fig. 3) and then fold the point backwards using the other dotted line (Fig. 4). Bring the point up again keeping both folds pressed (Fig. 5) and mark two upright lines, as shown, at equal distances from the corners A and B. Take A across to a spot on the bottom edge that will make a fold at the left-hand dotted line. Press that fold only as far up as the middle crease (Fig. 6) and do the same to B so that A and B can be held forward together (Fig. 7). Separate A and B as in Fig. 5 and turn the paper over (Fig. 8). Fold the bottom edge up, then over again, following the horizontal dotted lines (Fig. 9). Take B and A round to the back and the creases of Figs. 6 and 7 will cause the Christmas tree (Fig 10.) to take shape. Turn it over again (Fig. 11), lock the end of B into A, then gently flatten the folds at the back into the form required. If the 'tub' is slightly rounded the tree will stand up.

(This version of his Christmas tree was sent to Rupert by Mr Robert Harbin, the Origami Man.)

45

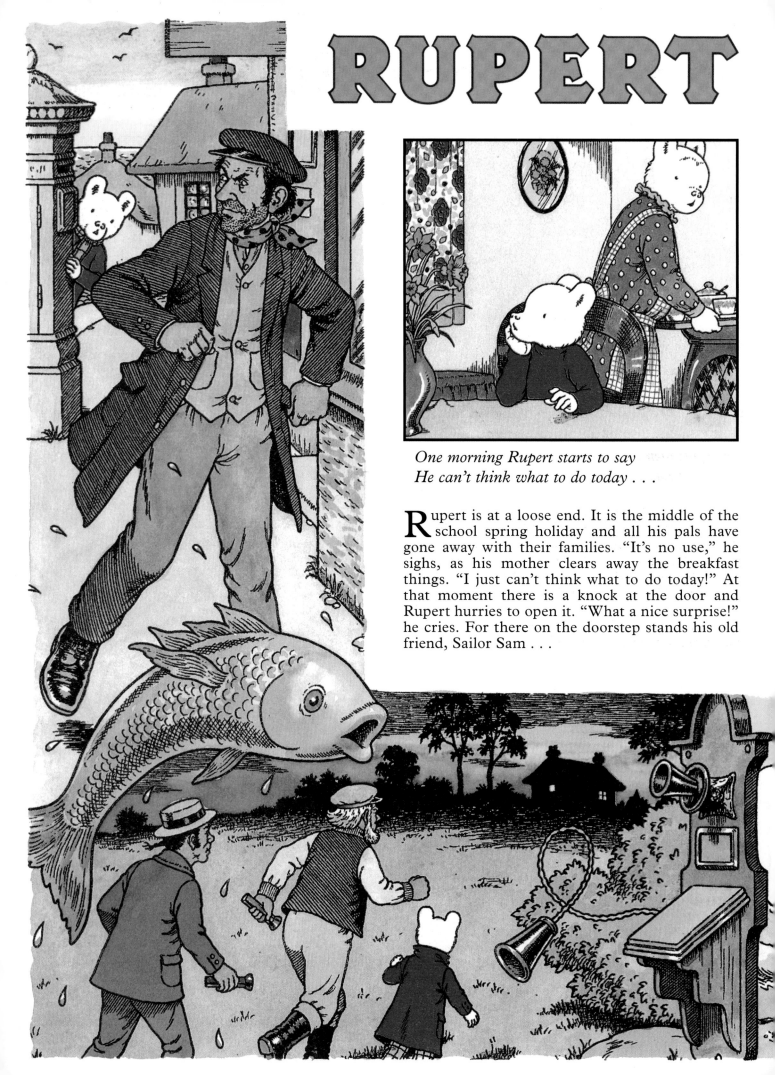

RUPERT

One morning Rupert starts to say
He can't think what to do today . . .

Rupert is at a loose end. It is the middle of the school spring holiday and all his pals have gone away with their families. "It's no use," he sighs, as his mother clears away the breakfast things. "I just can't think what to do today!" At that moment there is a knock at the door and Rupert hurries to open it. "What a nice surprise!" he cries. For there on the doorstep stands his old friend, Sailor Sam . . .

and the Angry Sea

But just then Sam, his sailor friend,
Appears and all his troubles end.

"I'm driving down to see the sea,
Perhaps you'd like to come with me?"

"How'd you like to spend a couple of days by the sea?" asks Sam. "I'm off to Cocklesands to visit an old shipmate of mine, called Jem. I've borrowed a car for the journey. Come and see." "What fun!" laughs Rupert. "I'd love to come. Let's go and ask Mummy." Mrs Bear likes Sam and knows he can be relied upon to take good care of Rupert. "Of course you may go," she says. "A trip to the seaside will make a pleasant change."

He asks his mum, then cries "Hooray!"
As Mrs Bear says that he may.

RUPERT SEES SOMETHING ODD

Sam starts the car, the trip's begun.
"Goodbye!" calls Mrs Bear. "Have fun!"

Near Cocklesands they glimpse the sea.
It's rough – although the day's wind-free.

"That's odd!" says Sam. "A false alarm!"
For now the sea has grown quite calm.

"But why are those two fishermen
Still hauling their boat back again?"

In no time at all Mrs Bear has packed a case for Rupert, and he is on his way to Cocklesands with Sam. Sam explains that his friend Jem is a fisherman who has a little boat of his own. Rupert can hardly wait for the sea to come in sight, but when it does, just outside Cocklesands, the two friends can hardly believe their eyes. Although it is a fine calm day the water looks windswept and rough. Then the road turns inland and they lose sight of the sea for a while.

When they see it again, from a hill above Cocklesands, they are even more surprised, for now it is still and calm! "This is mighty odd," says Sam. "All the boats should be out fishing by now. Yet there's only one in the water and even that's being beached." When they get closer Rupert and Sam can see that the two men who are dragging the boat ashore are soaked to the skin. "Let's find Jem and ask him what's going on," says Sam.

RUPERT HEARS A STRANGE TALE

They go to visit Sam's friend, Jem,
Who hurries out to welcome them.

"How's fishing?" asks Sam. "Stormy seas?"
"Yes," Jem replies. "Though not a breeze!"

"The moment boats put out to sea
It storms and rages fearfully!"

"One tried today, but, as you saw,
We had to winch it back ashore . . ."

Jem is standing at his cottage door when the two chums arrive. He shakes hands and admires Sam's car, but his eyes keep straying to the boat that's just been beached. Inside the cottage Sam asks him what's wrong. "It's plain you're worried about something," he says. "Ay, like all of us here," says Jem, adding, as if to himself, "'cept for one!" "Does it have to do with the sea?" asks Sam, remembering what he and Rupert have just seen. "That it has," sighs Jem.

He sits down at the table and begins to tell them what's been happening . . . "One fine day, the local fishing boats set out to sea as usual, but as they reached the entrance to the bay a great wind sprang up and drove them back towards the shore. Ever since then, no matter how calm it seems, the moment the boats reach the open sea a sudden squall forces them back again. We send a boat out early each day to see if things have changed but it was just the same this morning."

RUPERT IS SHOWN JONTY JINKS

"There's something very wrong, I fear,
That threatens everybody here."

" 'Cept Jonty Jinks, who says that he
No longer needs to fish the sea."

"Wake up," says Sam. "It's fine today.
Let's watch the boats down by the bay."

"Hello!" says Jonty Jinks. "Nice day –
At least, for now it looks that way!"

"It's as if the sea was angry with people here," Rupert suggests. "Ay, just so," agrees Jem. "And that's why everyone in Cocklesands is so worried." "All except one, you said," Rupert reminds him. "And there's the very one!" cries Jem, who has been looking out of the window. "Jonty Jinks himself!" The others follow his gaze to see a man who looks as if he's gloating over the idle boats. "Fisherman till lately," Jem adds. "But now he says he's giving it all up."

Next morning Rupert is woken early by Sam. It is a fine day. "They're taking a boat out to test the sea right after breakfast," Sam says. "Let's go and watch." And so a little later the two friends march down to the shore, together with Jem. When they get there two fishermen are pushing a boat into the water, watched by a small crowd. Jonty Jinks is there too but stands apart from the others. "Nice day," he says, then adds with a smirk, "For the moment, anyway."

RUPERT SEES A SUDDEN SQUALL

The fishermen watch anxiously
As the first boat puts out to sea . . .

At first all's well, but then, oh no!
A sudden storm begins to blow . . .

"Stay there!" calls Sam and hurries to
Do what he can to help the crew.

"No more of that for me!" says Jinks.
"I'll soon be rich!" he laughs, then winks.

The friends ignore Jinks, for everyone's attention is on the boat being launched into the calm sea. As the boat turns towards the entrance to the bay it starts to get rougher, not much, but more than you'd expect on such a fine day. Everyone – except Jinks – watches anxiously. The boat has almost reached the open sea when a groan goes up from the onlookers. In an instant the sea is whipped into a fury and the boat hurled back towards the shore.

"Stay there!" Sam shouts to Rupert, as he and Jem race to where the boat is about to be washed ashore with its crew drenched and gasping. Almost as if it's satisfied with having hurled back the boat, the sea grows calm once more. A voice behind Rupert says, "Makes me glad I can give up fishin'." It's Jonty Jinks. "How can you do that?" asks Rupert. "Surely it's your living?" Tapping his nose mysteriously, Jinks winks at him and says, "Comin' into money, I am. Lots of money!"

RUPERT EXPLORES THE SHORE

As Sam returns Jinks walks away
And Jem asks what he had to say.

Jem seems surprised by Jinks's news.
"What's made him rich?" he starts to muse.

Now that the sea is calm once more,
Rupert decides to search the shore.

Although the tide's a long way out
He sees something splashing about . . .

Jinks stalks away as Sam and Jem return from helping to pull the boat ashore. "Did I see that Jonty Jinks talking to you, Rupert?" asks Jem. "You know, he's none too well liked round here. What did he have to say?" "He was telling me he's coming into money," replies Rupert. "Is he now?" breathes Jem. "I wonder where that's coming from. No wonder he's been going about looking as if he hadn't a care and saying he's giving up the fishing!"

Sam and Jem look thoughtful. Seeing that they have lots of things to talk about, Rupert asks if he may go and explore the shore. Of course he can, he's told. But at the first sign of a squall, he must be sure to take shelter. So off he goes, heading for the rocks, where he hopes to find some interesting pools below the high tidemark. He is almost at the end of the bay when his eye is caught by a wild thrashing and splashing coming from a pool that's hidden by a cluster of rocks.

RUPERT FINDS A STRANDED FISH

"A fish!" gasps Rupert. "Goodness me!
It's been left stranded by the seal"

"There must be something I can do.
Yes! This pool's big enough for you."

The fish looks pleased and starts to swim
Around as Rupert watches him.

Then Rupert's shocked to hear it say,
"I should have known to stay away!"

Rupert steals up to the pool and peers in. To his surprise, he sees a big fish thrashing about in the shallow water. "Poor thing!" he cries. "It must have been stranded here by the sudden squall." Rupert decides to help the fish. The sea is too far out to risk carrying it to the water's edge, so he starts to look around for a bigger pool. As soon as he finds one, he goes back to the fish and explains what he's about to do. To his surprise, it lets him lift it out of the water and carry it to the bigger pool, as if it understood every word. "You should be all right here until high tide," Rupert says as the fish circles the pool. He gets the odd impression that the fish gives him a grateful glance. "I suppose you were washed up by the squall," he goes on. Even though it seems as if the fish understands him, Rupert nearly jumps out of his skin when it pokes its head out of the water and starts to speak. "It's all my own fault. I should have known to stay away!"

RUPERT RESCUES THE FISH

"King Neptune's cross and warned that he
Would stop boats putting out to sea!"

"The tide will soon come in again,
Perhaps you'd watch and tell me when?"

The fish leaps up and says, "The sea
Is nearer now, please carry me."

He cries "Thanks!" as they reach the shore
Then dives into the sea once more.

Rupert is still staring in amazement as the fish goes on: "I knew all fish had been warned to stay away from Cocklesands Bay because it was the target of our King Neptune's wrath. I wasn't told why, so I thought I'd come and take a look at the place. Should have known better! That squall was a bit of Neptune's wrath, all right! By the way, has the tide started to come in yet?" "It . . . it's coming in fast," stammers Rupert, still astonished to meet a talking fish! At this, the fish leaps out of the water and casts a glance at the incoming tide. "It's close enough for you to carry me back now," it says. "Just hold out your arms." Rupert does as he is asked. The fish jumps up into his outstretched arms and Rupert hurries towards the water's edge. "Before you go, tell me how it is you can talk," he asks the fish. "Learned how to from Sea Sprites and the like," it replies proudly. "Thanks for saving me!" it cries, and, with a final flick of its tail, it dives into the sea.

RUPERT TELLS THE FISH'S TALE

Rupert runs back to tell his tale
And why the fishing's bound to fail.

"A talking fish!" cries Jem. "Flimflam!"
"No, Rupert never fibs," says Sam.

But why is Neptune cross with them?
"Perhaps he's lost something?" says Jem.

They all decide that must be why,
Then Jonty Jinks goes walking by.

Rupert races back to tell Jem and Sam about the fish and what he has learned from it – that the squalls are a sign of King Neptune's anger with Cocklesands. It's plain that Jem doesn't believe a word of his story. At least, he doesn't until Sam says, "It may sound far-fetched, Jem, but I've known Rupert a long time and 'pon my word, he never tells fibs. If he says it happened, then it did. Besides, when I was at sea, I heard tales of Neptune's wrath – and of talking fish too."

"But why should Neptune be angry with Cocklesands?" cries Jem. "Perhaps someone has taken something valuable from the sea," suggests Sam. "He's got lots of precious things hidden away beneath the waves." But who in Cocklesands could have taken something valuable belonging to King Neptune? Rupert and the others are asking themselves this very question when Jonty Jinks comes strolling by. All at once, they find themselves thinking the same thing . . .

RUPERT SEES JINKS CHALLENGED

*"Jinks's new wealth!" cries Sam. "Could he
Have taken something from the sea?"*

*"Come back!" cries Jem. "Before you go,
There's something that I'd like to know . . ."*

*"This money that you say you're due –
You've found some treasure, haven't you!"*

*Jem's sure he's right, but Jinks won't say
He simply turns and walks away . . .*

''Jinks's new-found wealth!" cries Sam. "The money he says he's coming into soon! He was very mysterious about it when he spoke to young Rupert here." "Let's go and ask him about it, right now!" says Jem. "I don't suppose for a moment that he'll tell the truth, but it's worth a try, to find out what he's been up to!" He hurries out of the cottage and calls to Jinks. "Wait a minute, Jonty. We want a word with you . . ." Jinks spins round, guiltily. He looks startled, then gives a sickly grin as Jem and Sam draw near. "This money you say you've got coming to you – the windfall that will let you give up fishing – you've taken something precious from the sea, haven't you?" demands Jem. Jink's jaw drops in dismay, but he soon recovers and gives Jem a defiant stare. "'Tain't none of your business!" he blusters. "Nor anyone else in Cocklesands." With that he turns away sharply and scuttles up a flight of steps . . .

RUPERT OVERHEARS A CALL

"I wonder what the truth can be?"
Says Jem. "Oh dear, we're out of tea."

He asks Rupert to buy some more
And sends him to the village store.

Rupert stops suddenly and blinks,
For by the phone stands Jonty Jinks!

"See you tonight!" he hears him say
As Jinks hangs up and goes to pay.

"Let's talk about this over a cup of tea," says Jem and leads the way back to his cottage. When they get there, Sam is just starting to say that he's sure Jinks has taken something valuable from the sea when Jem discovers that the tea caddy is empty. "I'll go and fetch some more," offers Rupert. Jem gives him the money and follows him outside to point the way. "The shop's just up this lane," he says. "Keep going and you can't miss it. It's our post office too."

Cocklesands post office has the only telephone in the village. When Rupert arrives at the post office, he sees that someone's using it – Jonty Jinks! He is just in time to hear Jinks say, "Right then, you'll collect it tonight," before he hangs up. "He'll be coming out in a moment," thinks Rupert and looks around for a place to hide. As Jinks goes to pay, Rupert hears the postmistress say, "That was a Milchester number you rang, so it only counts as a local call."

RUPERT FINDS A PHONE NUMBER

Jinks leaves and Rupert wonders who
It was he heard him talking to?

Inside the shop, he's quick to find
Some paper that Jinks left behind.

Rupert unfolds the screwed-up note
And reads a number that Jinks wrote.

"Someone in Milchester, you say?"
Cries Sam, "Let's call them right away!"

Rupert hides behind a post-box as Jinks comes out of the shop and hurries away. He wonders if he should follow him, in the hope of learning more, then he remembers the tea he's been sent to buy and enters the shop instead. "Some people have no idea of tidiness!" complains the postmistress. "The man who just left simply threw that piece of paper on the floor!" Rupert scoops up the ball of paper she points to. "Don't worry, I'll get rid of it for you," he says.

Before the postmistress can say another word, Rupert asks her for the packet of tea. As soon as he gets outside, he unfolds the screwed-up piece of paper and finds what looks like a telephone number written on it. He hurries back to the others straightaway. "You say he was calling Milchester?" says Sam when Rupert tells him everything that happened. "Well, it's pretty clear that this is the number he was calling. Let's ring it right now and find out whose it is."

RUPERT'S FRIEND MAKES A CALL

Sam asks to use the phone and then
Calls the same number once again . . .

He soon rings off and quickly goes
To tell the others what he knows.

"Who was it?" Jem asks anxiously.
A man Sam's heard of – Sir Humphrey!

"The man that Jinks was talking to
Is famous for his private zoo!"

"The postmistress will find it odd if Rupert goes back to the shop so soon," Sam tells Jem. "You two stay here, while I go inside and make the call." "What a coincidence! You're the second person to ask for that number today," says the postmistress. "I'll just put you through." Sam looks grim as he hears the person who answers the 'phone. "Sorry, wrong number!" he says and hangs up quickly. "Who was it?" ask Rupert and Jem anxiously.

"Sir Humphrey Pumphrey!" exclaims Sam. "I've heard lots about him in my time, and none of it very good!" As the friends make their way back to Jem's cottage, Sam explains that Sir Humphrey is the owner of a private zoo, which only he is ever allowed to see. "'Tis said it contains very rare creatures, for which he has paid a lot of money! People bring him animals they've caught from all over the world – he's none too worried how they're come by!"

RUPERT JOINS A NIGHT WATCH

Back at Jem's cottage, all agree
He must want something from the sea!

"We've got to stop him if we can!"
Says Jem. "Wait here, I've got a plan!"

When Jem returns he says that they
Must go to Jinks's straightaway . . .

"He's meeting someone here tonight.
We'll watch but keep well out of sight."

Over a meal that evening, the friends all agree it must be a living thing that Jinks has taken from the sea if Sir Humphrey Pumphrey wants it. "And he's collecting it tonight," says Rupert. "That's what Jinks said on the 'phone." "Then we'll keep watch on Jinks's place as soon as it's dark," declares Jem. "But what can we do?" Rupert asks. "Leave that to me," says Jem. "I've got an idea!" Telling the others he'll be back later, he gets up and makes for the door.

It is dark when Jem returns. He apologises for having been gone so long but says there's no time to explain. "We've got to get up to Jinks's place straightaway!" he says. "Be sure to wrap up warm. We may have a long, cold wait." A few minutes later the three of them set off towards Jonty Jinks's home, warmly clad and carrying a couple of powerful torches. The cottage lies some distance from the village and as they draw near, they can see a bright light shining in the window.

RUPERT SEES JINKS AMBUSHED

"Hush!" whispers Jem. "Don't breathe a word!"
As an approaching car is heard.

A fat man knocks at Jinks's door –
Sir Humphrey Pumphrey! Sam is sure . . .

Jinks carries something to the car.
"This way," says Pumphrey. "It's not far!"

"Stay there!" Sam cries out suddenly.
"You've stolen something from the sea!"

Jem leads the way to a clump of bushes from which they can watch Jinks's cottage without being seen. For a long time nothing happens, but Rupert is sure he can hear something moving When he mentions it Jem says it's nothing and tells him to hush. At last, a car comes into sight. It pulls up outside the cottage and a large man gets out. He marches up to the front door, which is opened by Jinks. "Come in, Sir Humphrey," he greets his visitor. "It's in the bathtub."

Sir Humphrey disappears inside, but soon emerges, together with Jinks, who is carrying something wrapped in a blanket. "Quickly, let's get this to my place," growls Sir Humphrey. "Now!" Jem cries as the chums step out from hiding and shine torches at the two men. "Whatever you have there is going straight back into the sea, where it belongs!" snaps Sam. Jinks and Sir Humphrey are too startled to speak, but from the mysterious bundle comes what sounds like a stifled sob . . .

RUPERT LEARNS JINKS'S SECRET

"Out of my way, and make it quick!"
Sir Humphrey cries and waves his stick.

Jem whistles loud and at the sound
His fishermen friends gather round.

"They're everywhere!" Sir Humphrey blinks.
Sam takes the strange bundle from Jinks . . .

He can't believe what meets his eyes!
"A little merboy!" Rupert cries.

Sir Humphrey is the first to recover. "Don't know who you are," he snarls, "but that bundle is going to my home. Out of my way." He raises his heavy stick. Sam steps in front of Rupert, as Jem gives a shrill whistle. Next moment, Sir Humphrey and Jinks find themselves surrounded by a crowd of grim-faced fishermen, who suddenly emerge from hiding places all around the cottage. Nobody speaks as they move forward and start to close in on the wretched pair.

Now Rupert sees what Jem was up to when he went off on his own. He must have spent all afternoon arranging the ambush! Sir Humphrey looks all round, then lowers his stick. Without a word Sam takes the bundle from Jinks, lays it gently down and undoes the belt which holds the blanket in place. As the blanket is unfolded a great gasp goes up from everyone except the two rogues. "Who'd have believed it!" Sam marvels. "A merboy!" cries Rupert.

RUPERT COMFORTS THE MERBOY

"You'll soon be safe, back in the sea,"
Says Rupert, reassuringly.

"I meant no harm!" Jinks starts to say.
"He got caught in my nets one day!"

Jem stops him with an angry stare.
"Leave Cocklesands," he tells the pair.

"Thank you!" the Merboy says, "but now
I must get to the sea somehow . . ."

The merboy sits up and looks fearfully about him. "You're safe now," Rupert smiles. "You'll soon be back in the sea." "No wonder Neptune was so angry with us," breathes Sam. "He thought we'd stolen this merboy of his." The fishermen glare sternly at Sir Humphrey and the wretched Jinks. "I meant no harm," Jinks whines. "He got caught up in my nets and I couldn't resist the chance to make my fortune by selling him to a wealthy collector."

Rupert has never seen anyone look a stern as the fishermen do when they hear Jinks's tale. It is Jem who speaks for them all. "Leave Cocklesands at once!" he orders the crestfallen pair. "You can come back to collect your things," he tells Jinks. "But you, Sir Humphrey Pumphrey, don't come near here again!" The rogues look sheepish, then turn and scuttle away. "Thank you everyone," says a small voice. It is the Merboy speaking. "Now please put me back into the sea."

RUPERT SEES CALM SEAS RETURN

As Jem's boat nears the open sea
The Merboy dives in happily.

"Please give my thanks to everyone,
And Neptune's too, for what you've done!"

Next day the men watch nervously
As the first boat puts out to sea . . .

But soon they start to wave and cheer:
Neptune's forgiven them, it's clear.

They carry the merboy to Jem's boat and in next to no time the little craft is heading out across the bay. Jem explains that he daren't leave the bay for fear of Neptune's wrath. He asks the merboy to believe that no one in Cocklesands knew what Jinks was up to and reminds him of the part the local fishermen have played in his rescue. Before the merboy swims away he vows to tell Neptune that, far from being angry, he should be grateful to everyone in Cocklesands.

Next morning the whole village gathers to watch the first fishing boat put to sea. Rupert holds his breath as it reaches the edge of the bay but the sea remains calm and the breeze gentle. The men in the boat turn and wave happily as on it goes, further out to sea. The villagers give a rousing cheer and throw their hats into the air for joy. "Hooray!" laughs Rupert. "The merboy's kept his promise. Neptune's forgiven Cocklesands and everything's fine again." The End.

RUPERT®
and the
Christmas Ribbon

RUPERT HEARS A THUD

One very cold and windy night,
A thud wakes Rupert. What a fright!

When morning comes, he looks around.
What could have made that raucous sound?

His mother tells him, "All's not well.
Poor Gaffer Jarge slipped and fell."

They pack a basket full of treats:
Some Christmas goodies, fruits and sweets.

It's nearly Christmas, and snow falls all evening long. Outside, the wind whips round the house, but Rupert Bear is cosy in his bed. He is just drifting off to sleep, thinking happily of the sledging he'll do tomorrow with his friend Bill Badger, when suddenly – *thud!* A loud noise outside jolts him wide awake. "What was that?" Rupert cries. He peers out the window, but it's too dark to see. "Perhaps I'll find out in the morning."

When morning comes, Rupert tells his mummy about the mysterious sound. Mrs Bear heard it too, but there is something of greater concern. "The postman has just called, with a letter from Gaffer Jarge. He slipped on the ice and hurt his knee." Rupert is worried about his old friend, and his mother says they can visit him that day. Daddy Bear goes out to get a Christmas tree while and Rupert and his mummy pack a basket of treats.

RUPERT VISITS GAFFER JARGE

Then off they go, to see their friend,
To soothe him while he's on the mend.

They meet his chums. "Hullo!" Bill cries.
"We've heard about a big surprise!"

The bear says, "I'm curious too,
But first there's something I must do."

"We're here at last!" says Mummy Bear.
"There's Gaffer, resting in his chair!"

Mrs Bear packs some extra bandages as well. By now the basket is full and rather heavy. Rupert has an idea. "We can load this onto my sledge!" he exclaims. "I'll carry the tree in the wheelbarrow," Mr Bear adds, "and I shall bring some extra firewood too." The Bears bundle up in their warmest coats. As they trudge down the path by Nutwood Common, Rupert spies his friends Bill Badger and Algy Pug. "Happy Christmas!" Rupert calls out. "Say, Rupert," Algy begins, "we've just heard that Willie Mouse has found something at the far end of the Common." "What did he find?" Rupert asks. Bill replies, "Willie wouldn't tell us, other than to say it was most unusual. We're going there now to see for ourselves!" Rupert is curious, but first he wants to check on Gaffer Jarge with his parents. He promises his chums that he'll join them later, and the Bears continue on their way.

Rupert and the Christmas Ribbon
RUPERT WRAPS PRESENTS

"We've brought a tree!" calls Rupert Bear,
"And lots of Christmas treats to share!"

His Mummy makes a cup of tea,
While Rupert decorates the tree.

They prop up Gaffer comfortably,
And find a cushion for his knee.

Then Rupert settles on the spot,
To wrap the presents Gaffer bought.

Gaffer Jarge is very pleased to see them. And when Mr Bear shows him the Christmas tree they brought, the old countryman's face breaks into a wide smile. "How thoughtful you are!" he says. "Ever since I twisted my knee, I haven't been able to get ready for Christmas." "We can help with that!" Rupert tells him. "You just rest," Mrs Bear adds, "and I'll make us all a cup of tea." While Mrs Bear goes off to the Gaffer's kitchen, Rupert and his daddy dress the tree.

Mr Bear brings in more firewood, and Rupert finds an extra cushion for Gaffer Jarge's leg. The old man explains what happened: "I wasn't looking where I was going, and I slipped on an icy patch just outside my door. Fortunately, it's just a sprain, so it should heal soon. In the meantime, your visit has cheered me up a great deal!" Rupert is very glad to hear that. "Can I do anything else?" he offers. Gaffer Jarge needs help with his Christmas wrapping, so Rupert sets to work.

RUPERT MEETS WILLIE

The festive cottage, glowing bright,
Makes Gaffer marvel with delight.

"We're out of ribbon," Mummy sighs,
"And we could use some more supplies."

His mummy says, "I'll write this down.
Now here's a list to take to town."

Though Rupert has a job to do,
He'll come with Willie when he's through.

When the presents have been wrapped, Rupert helps Gaffer Jarge to his feet. They find Rupert's parents and a jolly sight meets their eyes! The room shimmers with colourful tinsel, stars and long paper chains. "I'll just tie this last chain up," says Mr Bear. "Would you pass me the ribbon?" "Oh dear, we're out of ribbon!" Mrs Bear replies. "I don't have any more," Gaffer Jarge sighs, "for I haven't been able to do any shopping all week."

"I could run to the shop," Rupert speaks up. "Yes, that's a great idea," says Mrs Bear. "In fact, there are a few things we need for our Christmas tea. I shall write you a list." Soon, Rupert Bear is on his way. As he comes into town, he nearly bumps into Willie Mouse! "Oh hello, Rupert! I've found something magnificent – come along with me now and I'll show you!" "I must go to the shop first," Rupert says. "I'll come and see afterwards . . ."

RUPERT GOES SHOPPING

So, keen to finish up his chore,
He goes inside the village store.

"I have the ribbon just for you,"
Says Mr Chimp. "Now will this do?"

He thanks him, then he turns to go,
And head back through the frosty snow.

"There's time," thinks Rupert. "Now's my chance.
I could just go and have a glance . . ."

Inside the village store, Mr Chimp reads through Rupert's shopping list. "Very good," says the grocer. He starts to gather the items from his shelves. When he reaches the end of the list, he pauses. "I'm afraid this is the only ribbon I have left," he says, as he shows Rupert a very large bobbin of bright red ribbon. As there isn't anything smaller for sale, Rupert agrees to buy it. "This could wrap all our Christmas gifts and more!" he laughs.

Rupert thanks Mr Chimp and wishes the grocer a very happy Christmas. Once again, the basket of supplies is quite heavy, so Rupert is glad to have his sledge with him to carry it. As the little bear starts down the snowy path back towards Gaffer Jarge's cottage, his thoughts drift to Willie Mouse and his mysterious discovery. "I do wonder what he's found that could be so exciting! Oh, perhaps I could just go and have a quick peek . . ."

RUPERT MEETS HIS CHUMS

He tears across the snowy ground,
To see this 'thing' his chum has found.

"There's Willie Mouse . . . and quite a crowd!
What can it be?" he thinks aloud.

The mouse calls to his friends below,
"I found this anchor in the snow!"

"The rope!" cries Rupert to his chum.
"Let's find out where this anchor's from!"

Having made up his mind, Rupert turns and speeds towards the far end of Nutwood Common to see what all the fuss is about. As he approaches, he can see several of his chums gathered there already. Algy Pug, Bill Badger and Edward Trunk are all looking up. The usually timid Willie Mouse seems to be perched high on top of something, his tail twitching with excitement. "That's not a tree or a rock," Rupert realises as he gets closer. "What could Willie be standing on?"

"Hello, Rupert!" calls Willie, and Rupert is finally close enough to see that the little mouse is standing on top of a large, golden anchor that's half-buried in the snow. "I found this anchor early this morning!" "But where did it come from?" Rupert asks. The others don't know, but Willie points to the anchor's long rope resting in the snow. "We were just about to follow the rope to see where it leads," Willie says. "It's this way, through the bushes!" Rupert exclaims.

RUPERT SPOTS A PLANE

The chums all are off! And with a push,
They clamber through the snowy bush.

Still following the anchor's chain,
They climb and spot a small toy plane.

It's Santa's toys, who cry, "Oh dear . . .
Our anchor's lost! It fell down here."

"It slipped down, with a thud last night!"
The bear responds, "Let's put this right!"

Rupert leaves his sledge by the anchor, and he leads the group through the snowy copse. The rope snakes around a bend and up the hill. "There's something there on the hill," Willie puffs as they climb. "Yes," Rupert agrees, "it's a tiny plane!" "But why should a plane need an anchor, and a tiny plane at that?" Bill poses. Then Rupert spots three small toy figures busying themselves with the end of the rope: a soldier, a cowboy and a clown. "Why, it's Santa's toys!" he cries.

"We're in a frightful mess here," the toy cowboy tells the chums. He explains how they'd tried to anchor Santa's castle in the sky to the ground last night when the snowstorm started. "So that's the anchor I found!" Willie speaks up. "Yes, but the rope came loose, and we can't work out how to get it back up to Santa's castle," the toy soldier replies miserably. "The rope is too heavy for our plane." But Rupert says excitedly, "I have an idea!"

RUPERT HAS AN IDEA

Along the hill, then through the hedge,
He hurries off to reach his sledge.

He runs back, starting to explain:
"Please take this ribbon for your plane!"

"The ribbon's long, but very light,
It could be perfect for your flight!"

He ties the ribbon on, with care.
The toys say, "Thank you, Rupert Bear!"

Rupert describes the large bobbin of ribbon that he bought earlier. "It's very long, but not as heavy as the rope. Perhaps if you tie one end to the plane and the other to the rope, you could fly up to the castle, and winch the rope up." The toys agree it is a good plan. There isn't any time to lose, so Rupert hurries back down the hill to the anchor, where his basket and sledge are safely waiting. It doesn't take long to return with the ribbon.

"You're right, this ribbon is much lighter than the rope!" the toy soldier cheers. Willie Mouse holds the frayed rope still so Rupert can attach one end of the ribbon. While he works, Rupert remembers the noise that awoke him last night. "I bet that came from the anchor when it fell," he thinks. Then Rupert carefully ties the other end to the little plane. "And we're off!" says the toy cowboy. "Thank you, Rupert Bear!"

The plane ascends. They hear a shout:
"Oh help! The clown has fallen out!"

They find the anchor. "Now jump on,
You'll follow where the plane has gone."

But as the anchor starts to rise,
It snags the basket of supplies!

Then Rupert lunges, without thought.
And soon finds that his coat is caught!

The little plane takes off, flying towards Santa's castle with the ribbon trailing behind. Suddenly, the chums hear a small cry. It's the poor toy clown – in the rush to take off, he fell over the side of the plane. "Are you all right?" Rupert asks. "I'm fine, but how do I get back up to Santa's castle now?" the clown says. Rupert thinks quickly, and replies, "You can ride up on the anchor. Hurry, you can still make it to the anchor!"

The chums race back to the anchor. The rope is already rising, dragging the anchor along. "Go now!" Rupert instructs. As the toy clown leaps onto the anchor, the handle of Rupert's basket catches on the other end. Not wanting to lose the supplies for his mummy, Rupert lunges for the basket. But the anchor wobbles and somehow snags Rupert's coat as well. "Rupert, no!" Bill cries, but it's too late! The anchor hauls the little bear up into the sky!

RUPERT FLIES TO SANTA'S CASTLE

"My basket!" Rupert gives a shout.
"Oh, everything is falling out!"

The little bear peeks down below,
At Nutwood, blanketed with snow.

And soon, they hear a jolly call,
From Santa, on his castle wall.

"Oh, ho! Who's this? Well, haul them in!"
And then greets Rupert with a grin.

By the time Rupert uprights himself, the anchor is soaring high above Nutwood. "I'm too far up to jump down," he breathes, "and my coat is still stuck!" The anchor swings this way and that, and the parcels in Rupert's basket tumble down to the ground. "My mummy won't be pleased," he says sadly. "Cheer up," the toy clown replies. "Your ribbon idea is working a treat! We must be close now, and Santa will know what to do!"

It's not long before the anchor is level with Santa's floating castle! Rupert marvels at the enormous turrets poking through the clouds. Atop the tallest one is another toy, cranking the handle of a large winch. "Steady . . . steady!" someone calls out in a deep voice. Rupert tilts his head and looks over to the side. It's Santa! The jolly man extends his hand to Rupert, and hauls the little bear in. "What brings you here, Rupert Bear?" he asked.

The bear explains how he got stuck,
And dropped his food. "What rotten luck!"

"I see," says Santa in reply.
There is a twinkle in his eye.

Along the walkway they all go,
With reindeer grazing down below.

"My storeroom is just over there.
It's this one!" Santa tells the bear.

"Well, it's a long story . . ." Rupert begins. The toys all gather round while Rupert recounts the day's events: Gaffer Jarge and his sprained ankle, the errand to find more ribbon, the discovery of the anchor, and how he ended up such a long way from home. "My family will be wondering what happened to me!" Rupert finishes. "But I've spilled all the supplies for my mummy." Santa smiles and says kindly, "I'm sure we can fix that!"

"You helped my toys return our anchor, and you rescued our friend the toy clown," Santa says gratefully. "I shall fly you back to Nutwood myself, but I must visit my toy storeroom first. Perhaps you'd like to come with me?" Rupert follows Santa along a bridge leading to the castle doors. He peeks over the edge, expecting to see more clouds. "Why . . . it's reindeer!" he says in awe. "Yes, that's their favourite grazing patch!" Santa chuckles.

RUPERT RECEIVES SPECIAL GIFTS

The storeroom's filled with Christmas toys,
With dazzling colours, lights and noise!

"Your ribbon trick has saved the day!
Please take this gift," the toys all say.

The clown adds, "One more thing for you:
A spool of ribbon. It's brand new!"

"I must get home," laughs Rupert Bear.
And Santa says, "I'll take you there."

Inside the castle, Santa opens a large door to reveal a storeroom with rows upon rows of shelves, each piled high with gifts. The tiny workers clamber up and down the ladder, carrying presents here and there. "We need help lifting these presents to the top shelf," says one worker after Santa introduces them. Rupert remembers the ribbon and suggests, "Why not build another winch here, and hoist the gifts up?" "That's a jolly good idea!" the worker replies.

The toy clown and toy cowboy each have a special gift for Rupert. "To thank you for all your help!" they announce. "We'll refill your basket with supplies for Gaffer Jarge," Santa adds. "He's very lucky to have such kind friends at Christmastime!" "Just one more thing . . ." calls the toy clown, and gives Rupert a shiny new spool of ribbon. "Now come with me, Rupert Bear," says Santa. "My reindeer need their rest, so I'll fly you down to Nutwood in my Santacopter."

RUPERT RETURNS TO NUTWOOD

The toys all cheer and wave good-bye,
As Santa takes off to the sky.

When Rupert's chums look up, they cheer!
So Santa chuckles, "Let's land here."

"I'd better join you, and explain,"
Laughs Santa, as they leave the plane.

It isn't long at all before,
They knock on Gaffer Jarge's door.

Rupert tucks the basket under his arm and straps himself in. Santa powers up the engine, and the rotors start to spin. Rupert waves goodbye as they rise. "Farewell! And Happy Christmas!" the toys chorus from down below. Santa guides the craft down towards Nutwood, and Rupert soon spots Nutwood Common. "There's my chums out sledging!" he exclaims, pointing down at Bill, Algy and Willie. "Look, they've brought my sledge back with them too," he says, relieved.

They're not far from Gaffer Jarge's cottage now, so Santa brings the craft down slowly. Rupert's friends have heard the rotors, and they rush over to see what's going on. "Why, it's Rupert!" says Algy. "Have you had another one of your adventures?" Bill laughs. Rupert would love to stay and chat with his friends, but his parents must be wondering about him. "I'd better come along to explain," says Santa. They walk through Gaffer's gate together, and Rupert knocks on the door.

RUPERT SHARES HIS ADVENTURES

They step inside and call, "Surprise!"
And Gaffer can't believe his eyes!

The old man says, "You'd honour me,
If you would stay for Christmas tea?"

The Bears and Santa all sit down,
And each puts on a Christmas crown.

Then Gaffer says, through happy tears,
"The best Christmas I've had in years!

"That must be Rupert, I do wonder what took him so long," his mother calls from inside. She opens the door. "Surprise! Look who it is!" Rupert exclaims. Mrs and Mr Bear are startled, but no one is more shocked than Gaffer Jarge, who stares up, speechless! Then Santa shakes his hand, and the old countryman finds his voice again. "Now this is something I never expected!" he chortles. "Let's sit down to tea," says Mrs Bear, "and Rupert can tell us about his adventure!"

Gaffer Jarge clears his throat and addresses Santa. "I'd be honoured if you would stay for tea," he says. "The pleasure is all mine," Santa replies. Rupert helps his parents lay the table while Gaffer Jarge and Santa swap stories of their favourite Christmases. The candlelight glows brightly, and everyone is having a very jolly time. "Thank you, Rupert Bear," Gaffer Jarge says. "I think this is the best Christmas I've had for years!"

Spot the Difference

It's a windy day and Rupert and his pals are having lots of fun in the garden. There are 8 differences between the two pictures. Can you spot them all?

HOW TO MAKE
RUPERT'S TOY CAMERA

This toy will give you lots of fun.

(You may need to ask an adult to help you with the scissors.) First cut a piece of thin springy card to the same size as the pattern on the right. Trace the shaped top piece on to your next card, then cut it out.

Next use a ruler to mark out the two inner panels, drawing dotted lines on three sides of each. Carefully cut round the dotted lines leaving the fourth side uncut to make two flaps. If you do not wish to cut up your annual, you can draw one yourself or take one from a magazine.

Fold back the card along the centre line so that the lower flap is behind the one with the picture on it (Fig. 1). At this stage colour your camera as in Fig. 1, and finish it off by gluing on a thin slice of cork as a "lens" and a scrap of cellophane as a "view-finder."

Now push back the picture flap and at the same time bring the red flap forward (Fig. 2) so that it covers the picture altogether as in Fig 3. Your camera is now ready. Hold the folded card at the top edges, then open them smartly, like a book. As you do so the red flap will slip back and the picture flap will appear – just as though you had taken a photograph!

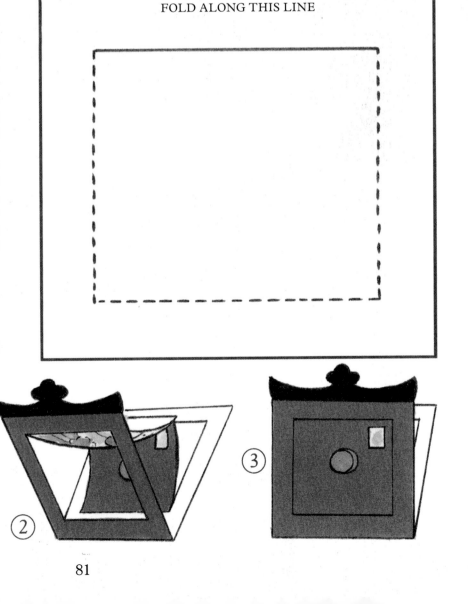

FOLD ALONG THIS LINE

①

CELLOPHANE

THIN SLICES OF CORK

②

③

RUPERT

The holidays have just begun
Rupert and Algy plan some fun . . .

They pack their rucksacks full, then take
A two-man tent towards the lake.

It is the beginning of the summer holidays. Rupert and Algy have been planning a boating trip together and are up bright and early, eager to start their expedition . . . "Have fun!" says Mrs Bear as she bids the pair farewell. "I've packed some food you can cook for your supper, when you set up camp for the night." "Thank you," says Algy, "We'll be hungry after a day on the river. It's hard work, paddling along . . ."

The chums' tent folds into a large bundle, which they carry between them across the fields. "It's wonderful!" laughs Rupert. "I can hardly believe we're setting off at last . . ." "Me neither!" says Algy. "In perfect weather too! Warm sunshine and not a cloud in the sky . . ." "There's the lake!" calls Rupert. "Down to the water's edge, then along the path to the boathouse . . ." "Hurrah!" cheers Algy. "We'll soon be there!"

82

and the Raft

John Harrold.

John Harrold.

"This way!" says Algy as he sees
The boathouse in amongst the trees.

"Hurrah!" cries Rupert. "Here's our boat!
Let's clear her out and get afloat . . ."

Rupert and Algy carry their load along a grassy path by the edge of the lake. "Not much further now!" puffs Algy as he spots the boathouse in amongst the trees . . . The two chums often go boating together and share a favourite canoe, which is stored inside for the winter. "Do you remember our last trip?" asks Rupert. "When we went all the way to Nutchester!" "Yes!" nods Algy. "That was fun . . . but this will be even better."

"Here she is!" says Rupert, pulling aside a heavy tarpaulin to reveal the old canoe. "Just the same as when we left her! The paddles should be underneath, together with a mug for bailing out . . ." "I hope we won't be needing that very often!" says Algy. "I'll help you fold the sheet, then we'll see about getting her into the water . . . It's always exciting when we launch the boat. It seems like the real start of Summer!"

RUPERT AND ALGY GO BOATING

The two pals stow their tent below,
Then clamber in - all set to go . . .

They paddle off without delay.
"Good! Now we're really underway!"

"There's Bingo!" Algy calls. "What's he
So busy making now? Let's see . . ."

Their chum explains he wants to make
A raft to sail on Nutwood's lake.

Launching their boat into the water, Rupert and Algy paddle out of the boathouse and moor by the water's edge. "I'll put the tent in, together with our packs," says Rupert. "If we balance it in the middle, we'll hardly know it's there . . ." Clambering into the canoe, the pair start paddling and soon get into their stride. "Steady as she goes!" calls Algy. "Right you are!" laughs Rupert. "We'll keep going till we reach the mouth of the river. It shouldn't take long now we're underway."

As Rupert and Algy paddle along, they suddenly hear the sound of someone hammering. "It's Bingo!" cries Algy. "He's over there, on the far side! I wonder what he's up to?" The chums paddle across to see and find their inventor friend busy at work on a makeshift raft. "Hello!" he smiles. "I thought *I'd* try a spot of boating too. Actually, this is the *second* raft I've made. If I still had the first one we could have paddled upstream together . . ."

RUPERT HEARS BINGO'S TALE

*"The first one I made looked just right
But then it vanished in the night!"*

*"The next day, all that I could find
Was this old rope it left behind . . ."*

*The pals tell Bingo they'll look out
For his raft, if it's still about.*

*They turn off from the lake and then
Resume their journey once again . . .*

The chums moor their boat and climb ashore to talk to Bingo. "Why do you have to build a second raft?" asks Rupert. "Whatever happened to the first?" "I wish I knew!" sighs the brainy pup. "I left it here, tied to a tree one night, and when I came back, the next day, it had completely disappeared!" Bingo shows the others how the rope he used to tether the raft has snapped in half. "It must have been a storm!" he shrugs. "If the raft broke free then it might have drifted anywhere."

Leaving Bingo to get on with his work, Rupert and Algy climb back into their boat and set off once again. "We'll keep an eye open for your *first* raft!" promises Rupert. "Someone might have found it, floating on the lake . . ." The chums keep paddling until they reach a narrow turning, off the main lake. "This is the way!" calls Rupert. "We can paddle upstream towards the source!" "I'll look out for a good spot to pitch the tent," says Algy. "We don't want to leave it too late!"

*"We need to find a camping site . . .
I think that grassy bank looks right."*

*"It's perfect!" Algy smiles. "Now we
Can pitch our tent and cook some tea."*

*He sets to work and soon the pair
Have supper in the open air.*

*"Let's check the map now, so we know
Exactly which way we should go."*

Paddling slowly along the stream, Rupert and Algy watch the sun sinking lower and lower, lighting the banks with a golden glow. "How about stopping there?" suggests Rupert. "Perfect!" says Algy. "We'll unpack the tent and set to work . . ." Rupert spreads the tent out carefully, then starts to fix the poles. "I hope I can remember how it goes!" he says. "It's a whole year since the last time I put up a tent." "Well done!" cheers Algy. "Now *I'll* cook some tea!"

Algy sets to work and soon has a pan of eggs and bacon sizzling on the fire. "Delicious!" says Rupert. "A day on the river gives you quite an appetite!" The chums sit talking till dark, then clamber into their sleeping bags. "Let's have a look at the map," suggests Rupert. "The river twists and turns so much, we ought to make sure we know the way." By the light of Algy's torch, the pair can see the whole of Nutwood's countryside, from familiar landmarks to far-off hills . . .

RUPERT IS WOKEN BY FROGS

Next morning, Rupert wakes to hear
A strange sound come from somewhere near . . .

He peers outside the tent and blinks.
"It's frogs! They're everywhere!" he thinks.

As Algy steps outside they all
Crowd round . . . More frogs take up the call!

Then, suddenly, the croaking ends
A big frog comes towards the friends . . .

Early next morning, Rupert and Algy are woken by a strange noise. "What's that?" gasps Algy. "It's getting louder and louder!" Rupert listens carefully. "Some sort of animal!" he declares. "It must be very close . . ." Untying the flaps of the tent, Rupert peers out cautiously, then gives an astonished cry. "Frogs!" he gasps. "They're all round the tent. As they catch sight of Rupert the frogs start croaking louder than ever. "How odd!" he thinks. "I wonder what they want?"

"What a din!" cries Algy as he climbs out to join Rupert. "I've never seen so many frogs . . ." The chums' tent is completely surrounded by frogs of all sizes, who keep up a rowdy chorus of croaking, which gets even louder as more and more frogs arrive. All of a sudden, the noise stops as a large frog, wearing a sash, approaches. The others all turn to him as if waiting for some sort of proclamation. "Do you think he's their leader?" whispers Algy. "I wonder?" says Rupert.

"Hello!" the frog declares. "I bring
An urgent summons from our King!"

"He needs your help. Please follow me.
I'll lead you to His Majesty . . ."

The pals set off along the shore
But can't guess where they're heading for . . .

"The King's Apartments are not far
But only frogs know where they are!"

"Greetings!" calls the large frog. "The news from our scouts was true, I see. They said two campers had been spotted by the riverbank . . ." "I'm sorry if we're in the way," starts Rupert but the frog cuts him short with a laugh. "No, no! We were *glad* to see your tent. The Frog King has sent me to ask for help with a very urgent problem." "Frog King?" blinks Rupert. "Yes," says the messenger. "His Majesty is anxious to meet you. Follow me and I'll lead the way."

Rupert and Algy follow the messenger along a riverside path. "I didn't even know there was a Frog King!" whispers Algy. "I wonder what he wants us to do?" "I don't know," says Rupert. "This way!" calls the frog. "The King's Residence is quite nearby . . ." Rupert can't imagine where the Messenger Frog is taking them. "I've never seen a palace near the river," he murmurs. "Not many have!" smiles the frog. "The Royal Quarters are hidden away where only we can find them."

RUPERT MEETS THE FROG KING

As Rupert walks along he sees
A lily pond, fringed by tall trees.

"This way!" the frog calls. "We can take
The floating path across the lake . . ."

Although the two chums hesitate
The lily pads can bear their weight!

The willows part and now the pair
Can see the Frog King sitting there . . .

To Rupert's surprise, the Messenger leads them away from the main river, to a small pond, covered in water lilies. Tall trees grow all around, with weeping willows stretching down to the water's edge. "Follow me closely!" orders the frog. "Tread exactly where I walk . . ." As the chums look on, he steps on to a lily pad and begins to walk calmly across the pond. "We can't do that!" gasps Algy. "They'll never support our weight!" "Let's try," says Rupert. "Perhaps they're a special kind . . ."

To Rupert and Algy's surprise, the lily pads hold their weight with ease. "They're just like stepping stones!" laughs Algy. The Messenger sets off across the pond towards a huge willow, which reaches right down to the surface of the water. Pushing through a leafy curtain, he gestures for Rupert and Algy to follow . . . "The King!" gasps Algy. On the far side of the lake, Rupert spots a regal figure, wearing a golden crown. The Messenger croaks a greeting, then points to the approaching pair.

RUPERT HEARS ABOUT THE RIVER

The Frog King greets his guests. "Thank you
For coming when I asked you to . . ."

"I need your help to find out why
The source of Nutwood's lake's run dry!"

'This marker pole is how we know
The water level's falling low . . ."

"It's got so bad I fear that we
Are faced with a catastrophe!"

The Frog King peers at the chums, then nods for them to step ashore. "Welcome!" he booms. "You come from Nutwood, I assume?" "That's right, Your Majesty," says Rupert. "We're on a boating trip along the river." "Excellent!" smiles the frog. "Sorry to interrupt your journey, but there's a threat to Nutwood Lake that frogs alone can't overcome." "A threat?" gasps Rupert. "What's wrong?" "It's drying up!" declares the King. "The level's sinking lower and lower . . ."

"The water level's been falling for days!" declares the King. "We measure it with this marker pole!" The Messenger Frog explains why the drop is so serious. "It's not just this pond that's fallen," he croaks. "Nutwood Lake's the same! They're all joined by a system of rivers and streams . . ." "We didn't see anything wrong," says Rupert. "You wouldn't!" says the frog. "That's why we use a marker. By the time folk start to notice it's too late. We need early warning while there's still time!"

RUPERT PROMISES TO HELP

The two pals tell the King that they
Will find out what's wrong straightaway.

The frogs who guide the chums all seem
To think the problem lies upstream . . .

With every step the level sinks –
"It's getting lower!" Algy blinks.

"The water has a single source
From which the river runs its course . . ."

The Frog King tells Rupert and Algy that nobody knows why the water level is falling. "That's why we need your help," he explains. "Unless the mystery's solved soon the ponds and rivers will start to dry up . . ." "That would be terrible!" says Rupert. "There must be something causing the drop, it's just a question of finding what's wrong . . ." The pair decide to start by following the river back to its source. "This way!" says the Messenger Frog. "Follow me . . ."

Following the Messenger Frog along the banks of the river, Rupert and Algy are shocked to see how low the water has fallen. "It seems to be getting worse!" gasps Algy. "Yes!" nods the frog. "I can't remember it being this low, even in last year's drought, when it didn't rain for weeks and weeks." The Messenger explains that the whole river system is fed by a single spring. "We should reach it soon," he croaks. "All we have to do is follow the course of the river as far as we can . . ."

RUPERT FINDS OUT WHAT IS WRONG

"A torrent used to fill this bed –
Now just a trickle flows instead!"

Ahead of them, the two pals see
An obstacle – what can it be?

"A gate!" cries Algy. "Somebody
Has blocked the flow deliberately!"

"It looks more like a capsized craft!"
The Messenger declares. "A raft?"

The Messenger Frog tells the chums that when the river is flowing in full spate the sound of the water is deafening. "It's only a trickle now!" thinks Rupert. "No wonder the level of Nutwood Lake has fallen!" Rounding a bend, the frog stares into the distance, then groans in dismay. "That's where the spring starts!" he explains. "It should be much higher than that . . ." "The river must be blocked!" says Rupert. "You're right!" says Algy. "I'm sure I can see something lying in the water . . ."

As the chums get nearer, they can see that the river is blocked by what looks like some sort of gate . . . "It's an old door!" cries Algy. "Someone's cut the water off deliberately!" At first Rupert thinks that his chum must be right, but as he looks more carefully, he realises what they've found . . . "It's a raft!" blinks the Messenger. "Most unusual to be this far upstream!" "It must have capsized," says Rupert. "The rocks are holding it fast and the water can't get through."

RUPERT UNBLOCKS THE STREAM

"It's Bingo's!" Rupert cries. "I'm sure –
The lost raft that he made before!"

"The mystery's over! Now we know
Why Nutwood's river's ceased to flow . . ."

The two pals lift the raft which blocks
The dammed up river from the rocks.

The frog lets out a joyful cry
To see the water rushing by . . .

The Messenger Frog is mystified by the abandoned raft, but Rupert suddenly realises where it must have come from. "It's Bingo's!" he cries. "The *first* raft he built. The one that was carried away in a storm . . ." Now the chums have discovered what's wrong, all that remains is for them to try to clear the river. "It won't be easy!" warns the frog. "Let's try!" Rupert tells Algy. "I'll cross over while you stay there." Taking a giant leap he hops across, landing safely on the far side.

As the Messenger looks on, Rupert and Algy take hold of the upturned raft. "Let's see if we can lift it clear," says Rupert. At first it seems impossible to shift but as the chums pull together it suddenly starts to move. "That's got it free of the rocks," calls Rupert. "Now let's try to unblock the stream . . ." The pair haul the raft out to the bank then peer down at the river, which rushes past in a sudden swell. "Hurrah!" cheers the Messenger. "Nutwood Lake is saved!"

RUPERT AND ALGY SET SAIL

*"Let's see if Bingo's raft will take
Us back downstream to Nutwood's lake . . ."*

*"We're off now! Hold tight everyone!"
Calls Algy to the frogs. "What fun!"*

*The pals' plan works – soon they can see
The Frog King's mighty willow tree . . .*

*"The river's back to normal now!
You two have saved the day – but how?"*

As they watch the river racing past, Rupert and Algy decide to use the abandoned raft to ride back to Nutwood . . . "There's plenty of room!" says Rupert, as he climbs aboard. The Messenger seems doubtful at first, but is soon persuaded by the other frogs, who are keen to have a ride. Algy holds the raft steady until everyone is ready, then jumps across to join Rupert. "Hold tight!" he calls. "We're off!" The raft gives a sudden lurch, then starts to speed downstream . . .

To Rupert's delight, the chums' plan works splendidly. The raft whizzes down the fast-flowing stream towards the frogs' special pond. "I can see the big willow!" calls Algy excitedly. "I wonder if the King's still there?" says Rupert. Although the raft has started to slow down, it still glides silently across the pond towards the curtain of leaves. As the chums push their way through, the Frog King looks up and blinks with astonishment to see that they are back so soon.

RUPERT IS THANKED BY THE KING

The Frog King marvels as he hears
The two pals' tale. "Well done!" he cheers.

He thanks the chums, "Without you two
We'd never have known what to do!"

The frogs all gather round and say
They'll help the pals' raft on its way . . .

Before long, Algy spots the place
Where they turned off from the main race.

"Bravo!" cheers the King when he hears how the chums cleared the river. "I saw the water start to rise but couldn't imagine what you'd done . . ." He looks at the raft and seems astonished that it made the journey all the way downstream. "An excellent way of travelling," enthuses the Messenger. "Perhaps we should have one for special expeditions!" laughs the King. "Thank you again for helping us solve the mystery," he tells Rupert. "We'd never have done it without you!"

Now that Nutwood Lake is back to normal, Rupert and Algy decide to return to their camp. "I wonder if we can sail back?" asks Algy. "We might," says Rupert, "but it won't be easy . . ." "Don't worry!" laughs the Frog King. "Climb aboard and leave the rest to us!" The chums step on to the raft and are immediately surrounded by a crowd of frogs, who offer to push them along. "You'll be there in no time!" calls the King. "Wonderful!" smiles Algy as the raft glides along.

RUPERT HEARS A CALL

The raft drifts on downstream and then
The two pals spot their tent again . . .

They thank the frogs and jump ashore –
Delighted to be back once more.

"Look!" Algy gives a startled cry –
The chums spot Bingo floating by . . .

"You've found my raft!" he blinks. "But where . . ."
"It's quite a story!" laugh the pair.

Following the course of the stream, Rupert and Algy soon spot their tent, half-hidden amongst the trees. "Our boat's still there too," says Rupert. "Let's try to moor the raft in the same spot." The frogs keep pushing until the chums reach the bank, then hop ashore for a final farewell. "It's our turn to thank *you* now," smiles Rupert. "We couldn't have had a better boating trip . . ." "I'll say!" laughs Algy as he ties up the raft. "Even though we left our boat behind."

Rupert and Algy are about to settle down to have breakfast when they suddenly spot another raft, travelling upstream. "Bingo!" calls Algy. "You'll never guess what we've found! Come and see . . ." The brainy pup can hardly believe his eyes when he spots the missing raft. "Amazing!" he blinks. "I thought it had gone forever!" "Wait till you hear the whole story!" laughs Rupert. "We'll tell you about it, over breakfast . . ."

How carefully can you colour these two pictures?

A PAGE TO COLOUR

RUPERT and the

It is early in January. For several days on end Rupert has been very, very good and the strain is beginning to tell. "I wonder how long New Year resolutions are supposed to last," he thinks. "I'll fetch the diary that Daddy gave me and see if that will tell me." But the little book makes no mention of it, and with a sigh he gets up. "My other resolution was to help somebody every day," he murmurs. "I'll ask Mummy if there is anything I can do."

He goes into the kitchen and finds Mrs Bear busily making a pie, and she smiles at his questions. "I'm glad you're keeping the New Year resolutions," she says, "but I can't think of anything that I want you to do at the moment." "H'm, that's awkward," Rupert sighs. "How can I help other people if they don't want to be helped? I'd better try to find somebody else." So he puts on his overcoat and scarf and asks if he may go out. At the corner he sees the figure of the old postman.

TRAIN JOURNEY

Says Rupert, "Now the New Year's past,
How long should resolutions last?"

"I've come to help you, if I may,
I must do something every day."

Says Mummy with a grateful smile,
"I've nothing for you yet awhile."

"Ah, there's the postman going by!
I'll help him, if he'll let me try."

RUPERT AMUSES THE POSTMAN

"I'll take the post and save your legs,
Please let me do it," Rupert begs.

The postman cries, "Well, I declare,
You are a willing little bear!"

"There's Mrs Pig. She does look bad.
I wonder what has made her sad."

Thanks Rupert, "Something's lost, I fear,
But what it is, I cannot hear."

Rupert hurries forward. "Please can I help you?" he calls. "One of my New Year resolutions is to help somebody every day. I'm sure I could take all those letters round while you go home and have a nice cup of tea." The postman gives a surprised smile. "Well, you are a nice little bear!" he chuckles. "But you don't understand. If I let anyone do my work for me I should lose my job altogether. Why not go and ask my cousin, Constable Growler, if you can be of any help?"

Thanking the postman for his suggestion, Rupert moves on to another part of the village, and very soon sees Constable Growler. "Hello, he's listening to Mrs Pig," mutters the little bear. "She seems very excited about something. I wonder if anything is wrong." He walks towards them slowly and is too polite to interrupt, hoping that he will get a chance soon to speak to Constable Growler. "I believe Mrs Pig has lost something," thinks Rupert. "She's unhappy."

RUPERT OFFERS TO FIND PODGY

"No, Rupert, I've no job for you,
There's nothing useful you can do."

"Please, can I help you?" Rupert cries.
And Mrs Pig stops in surprise.

Gasps Rupert, "Podgy's gone? Oh dear!
What ever made him disappear?"

He climbs a hill, and does not stop
Until at last he's at the top.

When Mrs Pig at length walks away Rupert hurries to ask if he can do anything to help Constable Growler. "So that's your new Year Resolution, is it?" says the constable. "I'm afraid you can't do any part of my job; you're too small." "Then I'll ask Mrs Pig," says Rupert. "She looked very anxious about something." So he moves away again, and soon Mrs Pig is listening to him in surprise. "Yes, you certainly can help me," she moans. "My little son Podgy has disappeared!" Rupert looks very worried to hear the news about his pal. "Where d'you think he has gone?" he asks. "I only wish I knew," sobs Mrs Pig. "All I know is that he wouldn't eat his breakfast, and now he has disappeared. Oh, I do wish you could find him for me." "I'll try at once," declares Rupert. "But I've no idea in which direction I ought to start." While Mrs Pig goes indoors he walks to a little hill which gives him a wide view.

RUPERT IS GUIDED BY FERDY

*"There's Ferdy!" Rupert cries. "I'll see
If he has any news for me."*

*"Well, you aren't looking very gay!
Have you seen Podgy pass this way?"*

*"Yes," Ferdy says, "he went straight by,
I heard him give a great big sigh."*

*"I think he's somewhere over there,"
The little fox tells Rupert Bear.*

Rupert can see nothing of Podgy, but he does spy a small figure sitting on a fence, and, running downhill, he finds it is Ferdy Fox. "Hullo, you're looking very gloomy," Rupert greets him. "What's the matter?" "It's this New Year resolution business," grumbles Ferdy. "My resolution was to not play tricks on anybody, and now it's an awful strain. Tell me, how long must New Year resolutions last?" "That's just what I wanted to know!" answers Rupert. "But my diary didn't say."

Ferdy gets off the fence. "Well, what was your resolution?" he demands. "One of them was to help somebody every day," Rupert answers. "And now I'm just helping Mrs Pig by trying to find Podgy who has disappeared." "In that case you're on the right track," cries Ferdy. "He passed here some time ago looking even more miserable than I was, and walking very slowly. I called, but he didn't trouble to answer. Come on, I can show you the sort of direction he took."

A robin, very gay and bright,
Chirps, "Follow Ferdy! He's quite right."

Thinks Rupert, "What can these things be
That Ferdy's pointing out to me?"

As Rupert runs behind the stone
He finds friend Podgy all alone.

"Now tell me why you ran away
And what is wrong with you today."

Ferdy leads Rupert quite a long way over the common and at length there is a pause. "We must be getting near the town of Nutchester," murmurs Rupert. "I wish I knew if we were on Podgy's trail." A robin on a tree hears him and pipes up with an answer. "Yes, I saw Podgy. He went just where Ferdy's going, so follow him." Thanking the bird, Rupert scampers after the little fox and finds him looking at two pointed shapes that have appeared over a boulder. Hurrying around the boulder Rupert and Ferdy find that the pointed things that they have seen are Podgy's ears. The little pig is leaning against the rock looking very tired and miserable. "Hi, get up," cries Rupert. "You can't sit there. It's too chilly and the grass is wet. You will catch a dreadful cold! How long have you been here?" When he is helped to his feet Podgy stands shivering with his eyes shut. "Now tell me," says Rupert. "Why have you run away and why have you come right out here?"

RUPERT'S CHUM IS HUNGRY

"I've had no breakfast yet, you see,"
Groans Podgy, leaning on a tree.

They help him so he can't fall down
And take him slowly to the town.

Poor Podgy feels so very weak,
He holds his head and does not speak.

They climb a ridge, and from that height,
The town at last comes into sight.

Podgy leans against a tree. "Oh dear," he moans. "It's my New Year resolution. I decided not to be greedy and I ran away because my breakfast looked so lovely and I didn't want to be tempted!" Rupert stares. "But, you noodle, it isn't being greedy to eat your breakfast!" he exclaims. "And it doesn't mean that you have to starve yourself. You're almost too weak to walk. Here, Ferdy, help me get him to the town. He must have some food." The little group does not move very quickly as Podgy is so weak that he has to keep stopping for a rest. "Our New Year resolutions seem to be making us all miserable," says Rupert. "It's very odd. I'm sure they're not supposed to act in that way." After crossing one more ridge many houses come in sight. "There's Nutchester," says Ferdy. "It's shorter to go there than Nutwood, but it's going to be a long walk home for Podgy. Let's hope we can make him stronger for the rest of the journey."

RUPERT BUYS SOME FOOD

And soon they all come to a stop
To gaze upon a lovely shop.

Says Rupert, "Let's sit down and eat.
Why, Ferdy! Won't you join my treat?"

"I'll get our tickets for the train,"
Says Ferdy. "You go back again."

Then Rupert turns, and gives a grin
As he sees Podgy tucking in!

Podgy looks rather uncertain as the three chums enter Nutchester, but when they stop and see the lovely things in a teashop window he agrees to Rupert's urging and allows himself to be led inside. "Come on, I've got some money left over from Christmas," says Rupert. "So we'll have a good meal and perhaps you'll feel better." He and Podgy settle down, but to their surprise Ferdy remains at the door, hesitating and looking at them thoughtfully. "Why are you waiting?" asks Rupert as he runs back to the door. "I've had an idea," says Ferdy. "I don't really want a meal, so I think I'll go to the station and find out if there is a train real soon and get tickets back to Nutwood. Then Podgy need not walk all the way back home." "That's topping of you," smiles Rupert. "I'll bring Podgy along later." Returning to the shop he finds Podgy tucking into a meal of tea and cakes, and looking much happier. "You're already looking better," remarks Rupert.

RUPERT ARRIVES JUST IN TIME

"You needed that, I told you so,"
Says Rupert, "now we'd better go."

They reach a road and cross with care,
First making sure no traffic's there.

Shouts Ferdy, waving to the chums,
"Be quick – before the next train comes!"

"Across the bridge! Just follow me!
Look, that's our train down there, you see!"

At last Podgy gives a satisfied sigh. "It's grand of you to give me that," he smiles. "I only hope it wasn't greedy of me to have such a good meal after my New Year resolution." "It can't be greedy to eat what you really need," declares Rupert. "Now let's get you home. Ferdy's gone ahead to the station to buy our tickets. Isn't it good of him?" They have to ask the way, then taking care to use a zebra crossing, they see the station ahead. As Rupert and Podgy approach the station their pal, Ferdy Fox, appears waving the tickets and dancing about in excitement. "You're just in time," he cries. "Can you hurry a bit more? I've got everything fixed and there's a train starting in about a minute's time." "What a bit of luck," says Rupert. "Which platform is it on?" "Don't ask questions, just follow me," says Ferdy. "How obliging he is!" murmurs Podgy. "It's not quite like him." They follow the little fox over a footbridge to the other side.

RUPERT FLASHES PAST NUTWOOD

Cries Ferdy Fox, "You must not lag,
That guard up there has waved his flag."

"But Ferdy, aren't you coming too?
If not, what are you going to do?"

Says Rupert, "That was rather queer,
But Nutwood station's getting near."

The train is travelling very fast,
And Nutwood station flashes past.

As the little party reaches the other platform, they hear the guard blowing his whistle and they spring forward. Ferdy quickly opens the door of the nearest carriage and hustles Rupert and Podgy inside. Then, to their surprise, he thrusts two tickets into Rupert's hand, slams the door again and stands quietly on the platform looking at them. "Hi, aren't you coming with us?" Rupert calls. "No, I feel quite fresh," says Ferdy. "It's a long walk back to Nutwood, but I shall enjoy it." And then the train moves off, while Ferdy stands on the platform watching the disappearing train with a curious smile. "He's behaving very strangely," says Podgy, "but this is certainly the quickest way home. Nutwood is the next station." The train gathers speed, faster and faster. "This is all wrong," mutters Rupert. "It should be slowing down." Then he gives a gasp of horror. "Here is Nutwood Station. We're not going to stop!"

RUPERT IS FAR FROM HOME

"We caught the non-stop train instead!"
Groans Rupert, as he holds his head.

When presently they clamber out
They're far from home, without a doubt.

While other folk rush to and fro,
The chums don't know which way to go.

"I wonder if that's our train there.
I hope it's right," says Rupert Bear.

The two pals gaze at each other in bewilderment. "Can the engine driver have made a mistake?" quavers Podgy. "No, I see it all now," Rupert sighs. "We got on this train just because Ferdy told us to. He must have given up his New Year resolution and started playing tricks again. He has been making inquiries and must have known that this train was a non-stop and not a slow one." For a long time they wait. Then another large town is reached and at last they can get out. Rupert and

Podgy are bewildered at the sight of so many people hurrying to and fro. "I wonder how to get back," says Rupert unhappily. "I've no money left." "Nor have I," murmurs Podgy. They ask if there is a train to Nutwood, and a busy porter points them up a staircase without looking at them. The stairs lead to a bridge across to another platform. "I wonder if this is right," says Rupert. "This platform is as quiet as the other one was noisy. There isn't a soul about!"

RUPERT CLIMBS INTO A WAGON

"Look, here's a wagon! In we get!
The train will not be going yet."

"We're right," says Rupert, "that is clear,
For Farmer Green's address is here!"

"The farmer's crate is very big,
And full of straw," says Podgy Pig.

Grins Podgy, "I'll make room for you,
So come on, Rupert! Get in too!"

Rupert and Podgy wander nervously up the platform. "We can ask the engine driver if he is going back to Nutwood," suggests the little bear. But the engine cab is empty. There is nobody to ask, so they stroll back, and Podgy inquisitively enters a goods wagon. After a pause Rupert follows. Suddenly he starts forward. "Look at this crate," he calls. "It's addressed to Farmer Green at Nutwood. Hooray! So this train will take us home." The relief of knowing that they are in the right train makes the little pals feel better. "We'd better stay around here," says Rupert. "The train must start some time." He examines with interest the inside of the crate, and then the other packets in the van. All at once a chuckle makes him turn. Podgy has scrambled into the crate, and is grinning cheerfully. "I say, this thing has nothing but straw in it. It's jolly comfortable, and it's warm, too. Why don't you come and join me, Rupert?" chuckles Podgy.

RUPERT HIDES IN A CRATE

"There's someone coming – let me hide!"
Gasps Rupert, as he jumps inside.

"He locked the door, I'm sure he did!"
Frowns Podgy, lifting up the lid.

So down into the straw they creep,
And Podgy soon falls fast asleep.

"If this is Nutwood, then we're back!"
Says Rupert, peering through a crack.

While Podgy is speaking there is the sound of approaching footsteps. "We mustn't be seen here!" gasps Rupert as he leaps for the crate and dives headfirst in beside his pal. "That's funny," mutters the man, "I thought I heard something go bump in this van." He peers inside, but all seems quiet, so, sliding the doors, he shuts and bars them. After a long pause the two friends lift the lid. "He didn't see us, and we're locked in," whispers Podgy. At that moment a shrill whistle blows, and with a jolting and a rattling the train rumbles away from the station, while the two pals find themselves gently rocked about in their straw bed. "I say," murmurs Podgy drowsily, "this is rather topping, so cosy and warm. I haven't felt so comfy for years." Rupert, too, settles down for a nap until more jostling and squeaking tells him the train has stopped. Scrambling from the create, he peers through a crack. "If this is Nutwood we must get out," he says.

RUPERT FOLLOWS THE PORTER

"The porter's come! I dare not stay!"
Gasps Rupert, as he hides away.

"He's closed the crate," thinks Rupert Bear,
"And poor old Podgy's still in there!"

The porter says, "This crate I'll shift,
But what a weight it is to lift!"

"He'll take the crate, without a doubt,
But first, I must let Podgy out."

As he pauses Rupert hears the doors being unbarred, and in a sudden panic lest the station is not Nutwood he darts behind some of the other goods. He is just in time, for the porter enters the van and looks around. "Ah, here's the crate for Nutwood," he says. "It's returned empty, but somebody has been careless; it's not properly fastened." And closing the hasp he pushes a piece of wood through the staple. "Oh dear, poor Podgy!" thinks Rupert anxiously. "Now he can't

get out!" The porter pushes the crate out of the van and drags it into position at the far side of the platform. "My, this is very heavy for an empty crate!" he grunts. "Perhaps it's made of extra solid wood." Rupert creeps to the door of the van and then follows him without being noticed until the porter stops to speak to a man in gaiters. "Oh dear, that's Farmer Green," says the little bear. "It's his crate, he'll be taking it away. Oh, please stop until I get Podgy out!"

RUPERT AND PODGY ARE PUZZLED

Then Rupert Bear tries to explain
Why both of them were on the train.

"I really can't believe my eyes!"
The farmer says, in great surprise.

Frowns Farmer Green, "Sit down, you two,
While we think what to do with you."

"You're safe in there, at any rate,
So back you go inside my crate."

"Why, it's young Rupert. Where have you come from?" demands Farmer Green. "Were you in that train?" "Please, Podgy and I have come from Nutchester," begins Rupert nervously, showing the tickets. "But that train isn't from Nutchester!" cries the porter. The little bear tries to explain their mistake without telling of Ferdy's trick, and at length the farmer unfastens the lid of the crate to reveal the worried face of Podgy gazing up out of the straw. "No wonder the crate felt heavy!" gasps the porter. The two friends are made to sit side by side facing Farmer Green, while he and the porter look very solemn and pretend to be thinking out what punishment should be given. At length the farmer can keep a straight face no more. "Well, well," he chuckles. "You young people must have enjoyed being in my crate. You shall have another journey in it." And, opening the lid, he lifts Podgy back into the straw and then pops Rupert in beside his mystified pal.

RUPERT HAS A BUMPY RIDE

Wails Podgy as he jolts and rocks,
"I don't like being in this box!"

They can't see where they're going yet,
But notice that the ground is wet.

Cries Mrs Pig, "That's Podgy's face!
Why is he in that funny place?"

"Was Podgy in there all the while?"
Asks P.C. Growler, with a smile.

Rupert and Podgy wait anxiously wondering what Farmer Green is going to do with them. First they feel the crate is being dragged about, and after a couple of bumps it is tilted up at an angle. Then a lot of little bumps tell them that they are being trundled away somewhere. "Whew, this isn't have as comfy as it was before," says Podgy. Rupert pushes gently at the lid, and to his great relief he finds it open. "Look, the ground's all wet," he whispers. "It must have rained while we were in the van." Without any warning, the strange journey ends with the crate being dropped flat and the lid opened. To Podgy's amazement, his mother and Constable Growler are standing beside them, and Mrs Pig is even more astonished to see him in such a queer place. In a moment he has scrambled across to her and gives her a hug, while the constable lifts Rupert out and smiles at him. "So, you've found the truant, little bear! Surely he wasn't in that crate all the time."

RUPERT FORGIVES THE FOX

There Mrs Pig and Podgy stand,
Once more together, hand in hand.

"Oh, Ferdy, you look such a sight,"
Grins Rupert, "but it serves you right!"

"Cheer up! I'll help you on your way,
And tell my tale another day."

Soon Rupert's home again, and there
He's welcomed back by Mrs Bear.

The chums tell their story, and after everyone has enjoyed it the porter trundles the crate away towards Farmer Green's house while the constable returns to his beat. Finally Rupert says good-bye and runs toward his own home. On his way he meets a bedraggled limping figure. "Why, it's Ferdy!" he cries "What ever has happened?" "Oh, dear, I wish I hadn't played that trick on you," moans the little fox. "I got the worst of it after all. I got caught in the rain, and now I'm soaked!" Rupert looks kindly as his mischievous pal. "Podgy and I had a long journey, but we're both home safely," he says. "You mustn't wait to hear it now. You're wet through, so I'll help you home." And very soon the little bear is alone and making for his own cottage. "Oh, what a time we've had!" he sighs happily, when he finds Mrs Bear. "And what do you think? I've kept both my New Year resolutions. And I still wonder how long they are supposed to last!"

RUPERT'S CHUMS LOSE THEIR WAY

Rupert and some of his pals have decided to plant a little tree to mark Simon's birthday, and each is bringing what they think will help. Most of them arrive early, but Podgy and Bingo, trying for a short cut, lose their way. "There's something strange about this place," says Podgy. "Who's that man talking to Constable Growler?"

"I believe that's a real pedlar," says Bingo. "My Grandpa used to tell me about them." He looks again, this time in surprise. "I say, there are lots of things here that start with the same letter," he remarks. "Pedlar begins with P, just as your name

does, and that's only one of them." "I think there are as many beginning with B, like your name," says Podgy. "Look, there is a boy, for a start. Let's count and see how many there are beginning with P or B."

Well, how many can you find? Why not ask a friend to join you, one pretending to be Podgy and the other Bingo? Then look at the picture on this page and see which of you can be the first to find nine things that start with the letter you have chosen.

RUPERT'S MEMORY GAME

After you have read all the stories in this book, you can play Rupert's fun Memory Game! Study the pictures below. Each is part of a bigger picture you will have seen in the stories. Can you answer the questions at the bottom of the page? Afterwards, check the stories to discover if you were right.

NOW TRY TO REMEMBER . . .

1. Where are Rupert and Rastus going?
2. Who are the chums hiding from?
3. What has Rupert received?
4. Who has joined the class?
5. Why is PC Growler smiling?
6. What is Jem describing?
7. Who is Jonty Jinks calling?
8. What has Rupert found?
9. What is Jonty Jinks carrying?
10. Where are the Bears going?
11. What is Rupert following?
12. Why is Rupert running?
13. Why has Rupert received a gift?
14. Why is Ferdy feeling down?
15. What is wrong with Podgy?
16. What has Ferdy done?

Follow **Rupert**
every day
in the
Daily Express